LILA'S LOVES

LAYLAH ROBERTS

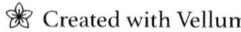

LET'S KEEP IN TOUCH!

Don't miss a new release, sign up to my newsletter for sneak peeks, deleted scenes and giveaways: https://landing.mailerlite.com/webforms/landing/p7l6g0

I now have a reader group! Want to join?
https://www.facebook.com/groups/386830425069911/

BOOKS BY LAYLAH ROBERTS

Doms of Decadence

Just for You, Sir

Forever Yours, Sir

For the Love of Sir

Sinfully Yours, Sir

Make me, Sir

A Taste of Sir

To Save Sir

Sir's Redemption

Reveal Me, Sir

Men of Orion

Worlds Apart

Cavan Gang

Rectify

Redemption

Redemption Valley

Audra's Awakening

Old-Fashioned Series

An Old-Fashioned Man

Two Old-Fashioned Men

Her Old-Fashioned Husband

Her Old-Fashioned Boss

His Old-Fashioned Love

An Old-Fashioned Christmas

Haven, Texas Series

Lila's Loves

Laken's Surrender

Saving Savannah

Molly's Man

Saxon's Soul

Mastered by Malone

WildeSide

Wilde

Sinclair

Luke

The Hunters

A Mate to Cherish

A Mate to Sacrifice

PROLOGUE

Lila shivered in the damp, dark alley. Drawing her legs up against her chest, she clasped her arms around her knees and rocked back and forth, trying to warm herself. Unfortunately, the rags she wore did little to protect her from the biting wind and wet ground.

But she couldn't go back. Not yet. Momma had a man in her room. As soon as Lila saw him enter the apartment, she'd escaped through the window and down the fire escape.

She didn't like that man.

She huddled into herself, wishing it wasn't so dark. The shadows looked like monsters, ready and waiting to pounce. Her teeth chattered so hard that pain pounded her jaw, making her face ache.

A flash of lightning lit the black sky, followed by angry, rolling thunder. Lila whimpered and placed her arms over her head as she buried her face against her raised knees. The skies opened and rained down on her, sharp and heavy.

"Get to cover boys, it's really coming down," a deep voice echoed across the alley. "Quick, under here."

Lila stiffened in shock at the deep voice. He had a strange accent, not unpleasant, his words coming out in a long, thick drawl.

"Where did that storm come from?" a younger voice asked. "How far is the hotel from here?"

Lila peered around the large garbage bin beside her to get a look at them. Three people were crowded under a large windowsill. And they looked large. Lila shrunk back into the shadows.

"Bet Gavin is laughing his head off, nice and dry in the hotel room," one of them grumbled.

"Hotel is a couple of blocks away," the man with the strange accent replied. "We'll just wait it out a bit."

Lila shivered, wishing they'd just go.

Lightning lit up the sky once more and she couldn't hold back her whimper. Fear flooded her, making her feel sick. She hated storms.

"What was that?"

Oh no, they'd heard her.

"Sounded like a dog or something," another one said.

Keep your eyes closed, she told herself. *Don't look up and they won't see you.*

"Jesus Christ, it's a little kid."

CLAY RICHARDS LOOKED DOWN at the scruffy child huddled on the dirty, damp ground and wanted to curse. He held his tongue, knowing he'd frighten the poor thing. And she already appeared terrified. Where were her parents? Why was she alone in an alley during a storm?

"A kid?" Colin asked. "What's she doing out here?"

The light from the street barely reached back here, but he could see she was tiny. She held her legs tight against her chest with thin, bare arms. She whimpered again, obviously completely terrified. And who could blame her? With the three of them looming over her. Short, dark hair lay plastered against her head.

"Stand back a bit, boys," Clay ordered quietly. His two foster sons immediately moved away. They'd lived with him for two years now. At thirteen and fifteen they were typical teenage boys; they grunted instead of using words, stayed up late and slept most of the day, and they left dirty dishes under their beds until science experiments started to form. But he wouldn't be without them.

Clay crouched down in front of the child, careful to move slowly.

"Hey there, sweetheart. What you doing out here?" he asked gently.

Thunder rumbled and the child jumped with a squeal. Large eyes looked up at him in fright.

"Don't be scared. It's only a bit of thunder," he told the child. How old was she? Hard to tell, but she was small; her face was too pale and thin, her body inadequately covered by her threadbare clothing. Where the hell was her family?

"Yeah," Colin said. "It's just God farting."

Trace groaned and Clay shook his head. That was Colin, always with a joke—usually a bad one.

The kid just stared at the three of them.

"Where are your parents, little one?" Clay asked.

The child continued to stare up at him silently.

"I'm Clay and these are my sons, Trace and Colin. I know we all look big and scary, but we're not going to hurt you. Will you tell me your name?"

She ran her eyes over him, settling on his hat. He smiled. "You like it?" Reaching up, Clay brought his hat off his head. "Helps keep the sun off in Texas. Although here in Chicago it's more useful for keeping the rain off." He placed the hat on the kid's head. "How about you keep it safe for me?"

The hat was too large for her small head, of course, but she tipped it back, still looking up at him. "Now, how about we get out of this alley and take you home?"

"I can't," she said in a soft voice. "Not until the man's finished."

"What man?" Clay asked, trying not to frown and frighten her more.

"The man with Momma. When he's gone she'll turn the light off, then on, and I can come home." The kid glanced up at a window further down the alley. Jesus, what kind of life did she live?

"He's been in there a long time," she said, sounding worried.

"Yeah?" Clay asked, trying to keep the fury he felt out of his voice. What kind of mother sent her tiny child to sit in a dark, damp alley while she entertained a boyfriend? How old could the kid be? "How about we go see your Momma?"

She shook her head. "Can't. Got to wait."

"I'm sure she won't mind, honey," Clay said soothingly.

"But the man will." Her terror kicked Clay in the stomach. "He's scary. He has mean eyes and he likes to hug me. He stares at me funny."

Dear God. The bafflement in that little voice betrayed her innocence. What kind of fucker was her mother hanging around with?

"Don't worry, sweetheart. I won't let him touch you." It was a vow. And he meant it.

The child glanced up, her too-old gaze taking Clay in before she looked over at Colin and Trace. He and the boys had been here a week now, visiting an old friend of Clay's. They were due to fly out tomorrow. As much as he'd enjoyed seeing Ian, Chicago was a long way from Texas, and Clay was eager to go home.

The city wasn't for him. He preferred the wide, open spaces of his ranch.

"You're big."

"That I am." He wondered if that was a good thing or not coming from someone so small.

"Okay, then."

Clay was silent for a moment. "Well, good." He held out his arms. She looked at them, then up at his face in confusion. "Will you let me carry you?"

He waited. Then two pale, thin limbs rose.

Clay carried the child up some rickety stairs, tucking her into his jacket. Poor little thing shook against his chest. Just cold? Or scared as well?

"Nobody is going to hurt you," Clay reassured the tiny child clinging to him, patting her back, horrified by how thin she felt. "I promise."

A small head nodded. "This is my door."

The apartment building was run down; only half the inside lights worked and the smell of sweaty bodies permeated the air, clogging his nostrils. He shifted her weight to one arm, holding her easily as he knocked on the door.

No answer.

He knocked again, louder. Damn, he had a bad feeling about this.

"Colin, come and hold her while I go check this out."

The child whimpered in his hold and held onto him tighter. Poor thing. "It's okay," Clay whispered. "I'll be right back."

Clay managed to untangle himself from the mass of limbs attached to him and entered the room.

Shit.

LILA DIDN'T LIKE the hospital. The lights were too bright and it smelled funny. The only thing that kept her here was the man holding her tightly on his lap.

Clay.

She still had his hat. She figured while she had it he wouldn't leave her; surely, he wouldn't leave his hat behind. She liked the way he smelled and the soft way he talked, even if he did sound kind of funny. She even liked the way he held her. He was big, but he hadn't hurt her or yelled at her or pushed her around. She wasn't so sure about his sons. They stared at her a lot and she wasn't sure why.

Something bad had happened to Momma. The mean man had done something; she knew he had. She whimpered, wondering what was happening. Clay tightened his hold. A warm feeling filled her.

"Why don't you two head back to the hotel room," Clay said to his sons. What were their names? Oh yeah, Colin and Trace. Colin was taller and he kept smiling at her. The other one didn't smile at all. "Gavin is back at the hotel and I don't know how long this will take us."

Who was Gavin?

Colin and Trace stared at her again before nodding. She was glad when they left and she buried her face against Clay's chest once more. It wasn't often that someone held her.

CLAY STOOD as the nurse approached, the kid still holding on tight. The only time she'd let go was when Clay had forced her to go to Colin, and he was glad he had. Seeing her mother in the state he'd found her, bloody and bruised, was not something a child needed to see.

"You're with Abigail West?" the nurse asked.

Clay nodded. He'd gotten that much out of the kid. Still didn't know her name though.

The nurse smiled at the girl. "And this is her daughter? What's your name, cutie?"

The girl looked up at Clay, who nodded.

"Lila West," she said quietly. "Is Momma sick?"

The nurse gave her a sympathetic look. "Come this way."

Clay followed the nurse, carrying Lila. Abigail West lay in the hospital bed, looking broken and worse for wear. Clay felt a surge of anger towards the bastard who'd done this. Abigail might not win any parenting prizes but surely, she didn't deserve this.

Her face was swollen, misshapen; one eye was so puffed up she couldn't even open it. She was going to be in a world of hurt for a while and who the hell was going to take care of little Lila while she got better?

Clay had already told the hospital he'd pay her bill; maybe he could offer to pay her rent while she recovered. She couldn't work for a while, that was sure, and Clay hated the thought of Lila going hungry.

He shifted her slightly so she was resting on one arm as he stepped forward. He didn't even consider letting her down. He'd always wanted kids, but had never met someone to have them with. And then the boys had come along. But they'd been teenagers when they'd come to live with him, beyond the stage of needing him to bandage their knees and read them bedtime stories.

Clay moved closer, still holding Lila who hadn't made a noise. Abigail opened her good eye, staring up at them. "W-who are you?"

"Name's Clay Richards, ma'am. I, ahh, encountered young Lila here and brought her home. I called for an ambulance when I found you."

"I can't afford this. Got no health insurance," she said her voice rough and hoarse sounding.

"That's okay, ma'am. It's taken care of."

"Well, good," she said harshly, a calculating look in her eye. "Maybe we can work out some sort of payment plan."

Clay knew she wasn't talking about money, and his stomach tightened in disgust. He let out a deep breath. The woman hadn't looked at Lila once.

"Ma'am, is there someone I can call for you? Someone who can help take care of you and Lila?"

The woman snorted, then groaned as she tried to move. "There ain't nobody who gives a shit about me and that good-for-nothing kid. Christ, what am I going to do? I can't exactly make a living like this."

Clay figured she wasn't making much of a living anyway. Lila shifted in his arms. Poor little mite, she hadn't once complained. He couldn't leave her here. He knew that.

"Ma'am, I think we need to talk. Just let me find someone to take care of Lila."

CLAY STEPPED into the dark hotel suite, hours later than he'd planned. Lila slept against his chest. All the lights were off except for one lamp in the living area. He'd gotten two connecting suites: Colin and Trace were in the one next door, while he and Gavin were sharing this one. The question was where to put the munchkin.

Well, first things first.

He needed to get her out of her clothes, well, rags. Walking through to his bedroom, he placed her on the bed.

"Clay," she said sleepily, rubbing at her eyes.

"Yeah, little bit?" he answered gently. God, how could that awful woman just give her up like that? Clay had offered to help her out until she was on her feet, to help her find a new job so she could take better care of Lila. The woman had laughed and said she didn't give a crap about the kid. That he could take her.

So he had. He knew it wasn't legal but no way would this little girl be going back. If he had to pay Abigail West off for the rest of her life, he would.

"Am I going to live with you?" she asked, looking up at him with calm eyes. Most kids would be crying or upset, not Lila. He worried about her reaction for a moment, and then decided she was probably just exhausted.

"You sure are." He quelled the voice in his head telling him all the ways this could backfire. Lila's mother got what she wanted and he got Lila out of that hellish situation.

"Where do you live?" she asked.

"On a big ranch in Texas. Colin and Trace live with me and so does my other son, Gavin who you'll meet in the morning. We have plenty of cattle and horses, even a few dogs, cats and chickens."

She bit her lip and sat up, her eyes huge in her too-small face. "I don't know anything about animals."

Clay pulled out one of his clean T-shirts for her to wear to bed. He stretched, his limbs feeling heavy and lethargic. Forty-six was too old to be awake at three in the morning. And Lila had to be even more tired. How much sleep did kids her age need anyway? How old was she?

"Lila, honey? How old are you?"

"Seven," she replied.

"Good, that's good," Clay said. "Do you need to go to the bathroom?"

She nodded shyly.

"Okay, you use it first. We'll grab showers in the morning. I think we both need some sleep right now."

"Clay?" she asked as she climbed off the bed.

"Yes?"

"Will I like it at your place?" she asked.

"I sure hope so. It's going to be your new home."

1

1 *6 years later*

A LOUD BANGING woke Lila instantly. With a gasp, she sat up, scooting against the wall behind her. Heart in her throat, she reached one trembling hand out for the bat she kept close by.

You could never be too careful in this neighborhood.

"Lila, open the door."

She froze. Oh fuck. Oh hell. It couldn't be. Her heart raced faster, but not out of fear now. What was he doing here?

"Lila," another voice added. "Open up or we're breaking this door down."

Lila groaned. Crap. They'd do it, too. She climbed off her bed, if you could call it that since it was just a worn mattress on the floor. She left the bat there. It wouldn't do her any good. Not against them. Never against family. And that's what they were despite the lack of blood tying them together.

Clay had made it very clear years ago that they were her family now. Forever. She'd wanted to believe him. Desperately. But there had always part of her that expected it to end. That Clay would eventually change his mind and kick her out.

Clay had saved her when he could have just left her in that alley and gone on happily with his life. Many people would have.

She'd tried to be perfect. Tried not to let Clay down. She'd been a model student, had done all that was asked of her, and had always worried that it wasn't enough, that she'd do something to ruin it.

Turning on the light, she walked over to the door in the one-room apartment and peered out the peephole. Only two of them had come, Colin and Trace. Disappointment filled her.

She was surprised Gavin wasn't with them; it wasn't like him to stay behind. The oldest of the three, Gavin was a take-charge sort of guy, plain-speaking and confident. He could be both terrifying and magnificent, making her feel safe one moment and then angry enough to kick him the next.

Damn, she missed him, missed all of them.

It had been six months since she'd seen them and she'd thought about them every day.

"Lila, stand on the opposite side of the room," Trace ordered. "We're coming in."

Okay, so their patience had come to an end.

"Wait, I'm opening it. I'm opening it." She wrenched open the door, staring up at Trace and Colin, standing shoulder to shoulder in the hallway.

"What do you think you're doing?" she asked in a frantic whisper. "You'll wake my neighbors."

"If they haven't come running by now, shorty, then they ain't coming. Now, be a good girl and invite us in," Trace told her. A slight frown wrinkled his forehead, but his eyes were filled with concern.

"What do you want? Why are you here?" She attempted to sound uninviting, even as she watched them hungrily. God, she loved them.

More than she should. She didn't love them like a sister should. She was *in love* with them. And the kicker was they didn't love her back. They were kind to her, tolerated her for Clay's sake, but they didn't love her. It was why she'd left. Staying would have brought her more heartbreak than she could have managed.

So she'd moved here to Phoenix. To be miserable and alone.

Colin ran his gaze over her, his eyes eating her up. At twenty-nine, he was two years younger than Trace and a few inches taller. Colin's deeply tanned skin went perfectly with his sun-kissed hair and deep brown eyes. The heat in those eyes sent a shiver down her spine. She was obviously imagining things. No way would Colin ever be interested in her.

Trace's bright green eyes watched her carefully, but with no less heat than his brother. They were looking at her like they wanted to eat her alive. Her insides clenched at the thought of both of them touching her, tasting her. Flushes of heat assailed her, weakening her knees. If she just reached out she'd be touching them. Just one small touch...

No! She had to stop this. It was why she had left. Because her attraction to them, to all of them, would never be reciprocated. Oh, they were nice to her, but they certainly didn't feel anything more towards her than brotherly affection.

If they had ever given her any indication that they wanted her, she wouldn't be here now. She would never have left. But when she'd told them she was moving out, they hadn't protested. In fact, they'd helped her pack. If that wasn't an indication of their feelings then she didn't know what was.

She cleared her throat. "What are you guys doing here?"

"Clay's in the hospital," Colin told her. "We've come to bring you home."

. . .

COLIN WATCHED as Lila's face grew pale. He reached out for her, worried she was going to faint dead away.

"Easy, baby," he murmured, picking her up and stepping inside the small apartment. She was so tiny, like a china doll. He barely felt her weight as he held her against his chest. God, had she been this tiny when they'd last seen her?

"Is he okay? What happened?" she finally asked, her gaze full of fear. She was even more gorgeous than he remembered. He knew she didn't realize how beautiful she was, with her mass of dark brown curls and those amazing hazel-colored eyes. Her plump, pink lips captured his attention and it took every ounce of control not to lean down and kiss her.

"It's not good," he told her. "The doctors don't think he's going to last much longer."

"W-what?" she gasped. He glanced around, taking in the mattress on the floor of the studio apartment, the lack of furniture and growled. What the hell?

He set her down on the mattress, and sat, facing her. Noting how pale she'd grown, he grabbed hold of her wrist, taking her pulse. It was too fast.

Shit. Way to break it to her easy, jerk.

Trace glared down at him. Yeah, he should have let Trace tell her like they'd agreed. Trace was way more tactful than he was. Colin tended to talk first, think later. He took a deep breath, watching as Lila tried to come to terms with what he'd told her.

"Okay, honey, I want you to take a couple of deep breaths and try to calm down. Can you get her a glass of water?" he asked Trace who was watching on in concern.

"Calm down? How can I calm down when Clay is...?" She swallowed heavily. Oh crap, he knew that look. Scooping her up, he ran for the bathroom and held her over the toilet as she heaved.

Colin supported her as Trace held back her hair. Sobs wracked her tiny body and his heart wrenched. They'd had over a week to get used to the idea of Clay dying and he still spent most nights fighting back tears. Clay was his father, his friend, his mentor. He couldn't lose him. And he knew Gavin and Trace felt as devastated as he did.

But for Lila this was a complete shock. She'd always been a tough little thing. She guarded her emotions. He could only remember her crying a few times. When her dog, Dastardly, died. When she'd fallen out of the large oak tree by the house and broken her collarbone. He could still remember his terror when he'd seen her lying on the ground, not moving.

As her heaving finished, Colin pulled her back and sat on the floor, holding her on his lap. Trace handed him a glass of water. Colin held it to her lips, ignoring her attempts to take it from him as he gave her a few sips.

Lila made another attempt to grab it. But he handed it back to Trace.

"Hey, I was still drinking that," she protested hoarsely.

"I want to make sure you can keep down those few sips first," Colin explained, resting the back of his hand on her forehead. "You feel a bit warm. Do you have a thermometer?"

She shook her head.

"Are you sick?" Trace asked her, crouching down to hand her a toothbrush. He'd squirted some toothpaste on it already.

Lila sighed. "Just a stomach virus or something, but I'm mostly over it now." She looked over her shoulder at Colin. "Are you going to let go of me so I can brush my teeth?"

He raised an eyebrow at her tone, which was damn well surly for her. Still, he supposed he'd be feeling pretty grouchy if he'd been woken in the middle of the night, told his foster dad was dying, then puked his guts out. He nodded at Trace who reached down and picked her up, holding her cradled against his chest.

"I can stand on my own," she said dryly.

Trace sent her a quick smile, but didn't answer. He set her down gently. She swayed slightly and Trace quickly grabbed her around the waist, supporting her as she brushed her teeth.

"I'll be waiting in the other room," Colin said. There was barely enough room in the bathroom for one person, let alone two over-sized men and one tiny female. He wandered out into the other room which served as a bedroom, living room, and kitchen.

And he didn't like what he saw. If any of them had known that Lila was living in these conditions, they'd have been here a long time ago, either to move her back home where she belonged or at least to a better apartment in a safer area of the city.

He would have come for her sooner, but they'd all promised Clay they would give her some space and time to be by herself, to grow up and experience life.

Hopefully his truck still had its tires by the time they left. He moved to the small kitchen area and looked in her cupboards, trying to find something to help settle her stomach.

God damn it, they were practically empty. Just a couple of potatoes and some rice. He knew Clay had often tried to give her money, but she'd always refused, saying she was doing fine.

Well, she was going to pay for that little lie. But not right now. She was in shock, she needed care, plus they still had to get her home.

"Trace, really, I can walk," she complained as Trace carried her back and placed her on the mattress. She immediately tried to stand, but Trace held her down, wagging his finger at her.

"Stay."

Colin's lips twitched as he opened the fridge. She didn't even have any milk. As a child, Lila had always gotten tummy aches and they'd discovered that warm milk helped settle her. It was obvious she hadn't been taking care of herself.

Well, no more. It was time for her to come home and let them look after her.

"Stay? Trace, I am not Snippet," she said, referring to Trace's dog, a part-collie, part-lab mix.

A sad look flashed over Trace's face, almost too quickly to be seen. But Lila must have noticed because she stiffened.

"What happened? What's wrong?" she asked

"Snippet died a few months ago, baby," Trace said gently as Colin moved towards them.

Tears rolled down her cheeks as she stared at them from large, grief-stricken blue eyes. Not really grief over Snippet, Colin knew, although she had loved Trace's dog. Sobs racked her body as both men knelt beside her, sandwiching her between them.

"What's wrong with Clay?" she cried.

"Pancreatic cancer, baby. They caught it too late," Trace told her.

"Why didn't he tell me?" she wailed, shaking hard. They held her tight, supporting her.

"He didn't tell any of us until things got really bad about a week ago," Trace replied.

She swiped at her eyes with the back of her hands, a childish movement that almost made him smile.

"Why didn't you guys tell me?"

"Gavin tried calling you," Colin said. "You never answered your phone or called us back."

Colin rose and grabbed another glass of water as well as some toilet paper. He wiped her face and held the toilet paper up to her nose.

"Blow," he demanded.

She gaped at him, unable to reach for the toilet paper herself because Trace held onto her tightly, keeping her arms trapped against her body.

"Lila," Colin warned.

Blushing, she blew her nose and Colin wiped her up, helping her take a drink of water. When she was finished, she slumped against Trace, obviously exhausted.

"How much longer does he have?" she asked in a raspy voice.

Colin brushed her hair off her face. She'd let it grow longer so it almost reached her shoulders now. "They can't tell us for sure, but not long."

"I need to see him."

"We know, Lila," Colin said, kissing her forehead, breathing in her clean, pure scent. "We'll get you there. Just lie here and let us do the work."

Lila slumped back on the mattress when he let her go, her eyes closing, her small body curling in on itself, as though cold. He glanced down at her too-pale face. She sported large, dark bruises under her eyes, as though she hadn't been sleeping.

When Clay had first brought her home, Colin had thought he was crazy. Not that Colin had wanted to leave her in that alley, but he hadn't expected Clay to adopt her either. None of them had any experience with children, and suddenly, their all-male household had been invaded by a tiny seven-year-old with huge eyes that seemed to see way too much.

At thirteen he'd been a bit selfish and hadn't wanted to share Clay with anyone but his brothers. He'd liked life the way it was in their testosterone-filled house and he'd figured a kid would just annoy him and get in his way. Plus she was a girl and he couldn't even teach her cool stuff like how to hunt and fish.

Boy, had he been wrong. Lila had always tried to mimic them, wanting to do exactly what they did. She hadn't been a typical kid. She'd been way more mature and well-behaved than any seven-year-old should be.

"Jesus, this is where she's been living?" Trace muttered to Colin, running his hand over his shaven head. They worked together, packing up her stuff. "I thought the neighborhood was bad enough, but this apartment is the pits."

"It's all I could afford," she defended, opening her eyes tiredly. She coughed.

"So we can see. No wonder you've been sick. Sleeping on a mattress on the floor in a damp apartment isn't healthy. You're lighter than a cloud and twice as pale," Colin said with a glare.

"Jeez, you guys are all compliments," she told them.

Colin held back his grin, not wanting to encourage her sarcastic tone. By now, he and Trace had packed most of her stuff.

"Lila, we need to talk to you about something before we go back to Haven." Colin crouched down in front of her, raising her face up so she was looking at him. He needed to make sure she fully understood what he was about to tell her.

"You grew up in Haven, you know the rules. You'll be under our protection this time. If you disobey us, lie to us, fail to call us when you need us then you will face the consequences."

Her eyes widened with surprise and some trepidation. But he couldn't back away, it was too important. At the core of their community was the belief that their women were to be cherished and protected.

There were a number of ménage relationships in Haven, so Gavin, Trace and Colin knew that their interest in Lila wouldn't be seen as unusual. Their greatest resistance would likely come from Lila herself. But that was something to worry about later. First, they had to get her home.

"We wouldn't hesitate to spank your butt if you put yourself in harm's way or risked your health," Trace told her.

She blushed, her fingers playing with the bed covers. "But I'm a grown woman."

Trace crouched down and cupped her cheeks between his palms. "You'll be safe; you'll be cared for and protected. Trust us to look after you. This isn't about who is stronger or older, or some ego trip. We care about you and you know we would never harm you. But if you put yourself at risk, then we won't hesitate in making sure you think twice before doing anything like that again. Understand?"

Lila stared at Trace, and Colin could see the shock on her face. Didn't she know how much she meant to them? Maybe not, and it wasn't as though they'd ever told her. But that would soon change.

She looked at them both for a long moment before nodding. "Okay, I understand."

A surge of relief ran through Colin, and, leaving Trace to grab the bags, he lifted her up into his arms.

"Let me down, Colin!" she demanded, wriggling.

"No," he told her. "If I let you down you might disappear on me." He needed her close, to reassure himself that she was really in his arms.

She was theirs. Whether she knew it or not.

"Stop wriggling," he ordered firmly. "I'm not letting you go." *Not ever.*

Leaning down, he kissed her on the forehead as Trace prowled around the small, run-down apartment, looking for anything they'd missed. This place wasn't fit for their dogs, let alone the woman who would be their wife.

Surprisingly, it was also kind of messy. Lila had always been a bit of a neat-freak, but there were clothes scattered around the place, a dirty coffee cup on the kitchen counter, and some papers thrown about, most of them overdue bills. He looked at Trace, then nodded his head at them. Trace gathered them up. They'd take care of them later.

"These walls are damp," Trace stated.

Colin scowled. No wonder she was sick. "How long you been sick, Lila?"

She shrugged, her eyes closed as she rested against his chest. "A few weeks."

Hmm, that seemed a long time to be sick with a simple virus. "I'm fine now."

"Yeah you look real fine," Colin answered her. "Let's hurry, so we can get you home where we can take proper care of you."

TRACE LOOKED DOWN at the small woman nearly asleep in Colin's arms. She might be twenty-three, but she was so tiny and vulnerable-looking that she could have passed for younger. God, he loved her. He'd loved her for a long time, his feelings towards her not the least bit brotherly. He'd felt guilty about that for a long time, until he'd realized that Gavin and Colin felt the same.

The three of them had decided long ago that they wanted to share a woman. Not conventional, but then they'd never been overly concerned with what others thought. And it wasn't like they would be the only ménage relationship in Haven. The three of them had built a strong relationship when they'd banded together in the foster home and none of them could stand the idea of living apart.

When Trace and Colin's parents died they were sent to a foster home. Clay, their father's best friend, had been overseas at the time. Trace and Colin met Gavin in the foster home. By the time Clay came for them, the three of them were close friends. The two of them didn't want to leave without Gavin.

So he took them all home.

Discovering that Colin and Gavin felt the same way he did about Lila had both surprised and relieved Trace. By then she'd been in college and they'd spent many nights talking, dreaming, scheming. Whenever she'd come home for the holidays, they'd done their best to avoid her, not wanting to risk temptation, knowing she was too young for them yet.

They'd pushed her away, which he now knew had been the wrong thing to do. They had hurt her when that was the last thing any of them wanted. After Clay realized what was going on, he'd sat them all down for a chat. Their foster dad had been furious and worried. He'd made the three of them swear not to touch her until she'd had some time to live a bit. He'd also made them promise to stop acting like assholes when she was around. Not that she'd come home much since.

But that was then. She was older now, though, and they didn't intend to hold back any longer.

H*ere to bring you home.*

The words echoed around Lila's brain. They were taking her home.

Clay had done his best to make her feel at home, even painting her bedroom in soft pink, buying the girliest furnishings he could find. She'd never had the heart to tell him that she hated pink.

She'd never been one to worry over clothes or make-up or the way she looked. Growing up with four men, she'd become a bit of a tomboy and that didn't worry her in the slightest.

"Hey, I need to get dressed," she complained as Colin started for the door. "And I can walk."

"We've got a long drive ahead of us. You might as well sleep for most of it," Colin replied.

"And what about when we stop?" she asked. "You expect me to walk around in my pajamas?"

Colin sighed, then set her down. "Fine, grab something out of your bag. But hurry up, I want to get back on the road."

Lila knew they would have flown if she hadn't been so terrified of flying. The first and only time she'd ever been in an airplane was when Clay had brought her back from Chicago to his large ranch in Texas. That had been an experience she never wanted to repeat. She'd spent most of the flight curled up in Clay's lap with her eyes screwed shut.

But Clay had never lost patience with her. He just held her hand and talked to her quietly.

She climbed into some old sweatpants and a T-shirt, then threw on her favorite sweater. Stepping back into the room, she found the guys waiting patiently. Trace had her suitcase in one hand and Colin held Tubby.

She blushed. Clay had bought Tubby at the airport gift shop before their flight left, hoping he'd help with her nerves. Big, brown, and ugly as sin, Tubby was the first and best present she'd ever received.

"Umm, I'm ready."

Colin came towards her and picked her up. He held her against his chest, handing her Tubby, which she took gratefully. She figured it was kind of childish to be so attached to a bear, but she loved the soft, worn toy.

"Colin! You don't need to carry me everywhere!" she protested as they locked up and left.

He grinned down at her. "But I like carrying you. Reminds me of when we first got you. I don't think you walked more than a few steps around the house that first year. You spent most of your time in Clay's arms."

Although he was exaggerating, it was true that for that first year she'd been almost afraid to let Clay out of her sight and he'd taken to carrying her around, her legs too short to keep up with him.

Unfortunately, although she'd grown, her legs were still embarrassingly short.

"Besides, you're tired and you don't need to be walking around in the cold when you're sick."

"I'm not sick," she insisted.

"Uh-huh, well, you keep telling yourself that, Lila. But I can hear you wheezing."

Trace beeped open Colin's truck and opened the back door.

Colin set her in the back seat and fastened the seatbelt. They were the most over-protective men she'd ever met and damned if that didn't make her feel the slightest bit warm inside.

"I'm not a child, you know. You guys seem to forget I'm an adult now."

Colin climbed into the front seat as Trace turned to look at her. "We know, baby. Hell, even when you were a kid, you acted so grown up. You never threw a tantrum or broke the rules or did anything bratty."

Now she was confused. "You sound disappointed. Isn't that what most parents want? A child who behaves and does as they're told?"

"Was that why you tried to be so perfect?" Colin asked. "Because you thought that was what Clay wanted?"

She swallowed as she realized how close he was to the truth.

"Is it that you didn't feel safe enough to act out? Did you think Clay would get rid of you if you misbehaved?" he continued.

"I-I feel tired now. I'm going to sleep." Okay, so she was taking the coward's way out. But she just didn't feel up to dealing with anything more tonight.

Luckily, they fell quiet, letting her drift as Colin drove them out of the city and towards Haven. Towards home.

2

"Lila. Lila. Wake up now, honey."

"Go away, I'm sleeping," she said grouchily. She'd been having the best dream. Gavin, Trace and Colin were with her, and they said that they loved her and wanted her to stay with them.

Forever.

She sighed in pleasure. A low chuckle filled the air and she realized she wasn't lying in her bed. She opened her eyes, sitting forward with a whoosh as she gasped.

"Where am I?" she cried out fearfully. She hated waking up quickly, especially in a place she didn't know.

"Shh, shh, you're fine." Trace stood over her, his voice gentle as he ran his hand up and down her arm. "Calm down now, sweetheart. Good girl. You're safe. I have you."

Lila slumped back against the car seat, taking deep breaths to slow her heartbeat. Colin and Trace were taking her home because Clay was sick.

Dying.

Dear Lord, what would she do without him? He was her father

in every sense of the word and when he died she'd have no one. How could he be dying? There were so many things she had to tell him, things she thought she would have a lifetime to say.

"Come on, little bit," Trace said, "time for some breakfast."

Lila looked around and realized they were in the parking lot of a small diner. Trace reached over and undid her seatbelt as she looked at her watch. 9:45 am. Wow, she'd actually gotten a few hours of uninterrupted sleep.

"Where's Colin?" she asked with a yawn as Trace helped her down. Despite the sleep she'd had, she seemed to feel even more tired.

"He just popped over to the drug store across the road."

Lila coughed and rubbed her chest, grateful the worst of the virus was over. She hadn't been able to sleep for the past few weeks, coughing her lungs out instead most of the night.

Trace took her hand, leading her like a child to the diner. Lila was too tired to complain, unable to stop yawning as they entered.

"I'm going to use the bathroom," she said.

Instead of letting her go, Trace led toward the lady's room entrance patting her on the bottom as she swung the door open.

She entered the bathroom, using the toilet before tidying herself up. Her hair was a fright—curls tangled into a mess. She tried her best to tame them with her fingers.

Still sleepy, she wandered out and saw Colin and Trace sitting in a corner booth. Damn, they were gorgeous. Handsome, sexy, confident. To top it off, they were good guys. A waitress stood talking and laughing with them. No matter where they were, women were drawn to Colin's easy smile and Trace's intense focus.

The waitress left as someone called out to her from the counter. Colin stood as she approached and she scooted in so she sat in the middle of them.

"Morning, Lila," Colin said, smacking her on the forehead with a sloppy kiss as she giggled and tried to avoid him.

She stilled, immediately sobering. What she was doing, laughing and playing around when Clay was lying in a hospital bed?

Trace grabbed her hand, squeezing it tight. "It's okay to laugh," he said, at once understanding what was wrong. Where Clay, Gavin and Colin had often struggled to understand what was going on with her, Trace had the ability to read her like a book. Sometimes it wasn't always a good thing.

"No, it's not," she said. "All this time Clay's been fighting for his life and I've been going on just living my life, carrying on without a care in the world. I have no right to have fun."

Colin grabbed her other hand. "Lila, you didn't know. None of us did. This is the way Clay wanted things and the last thing he would want is for you to stop living your life. Not that you seemed to have much of a life in that dump. Why exactly were you living in that apartment with no furniture or food? What happened to your job?"

Lila was grateful that another waitress chose that moment to come up to them.

"Morning, what can I get for ya?" she asked, smacking some gum between her teeth.

"I'll have the special," Colin said. "And coffee."

"Same for me," Trace spoke up.

"I'll just have coffee," Lila ordered. She didn't like to eat much in the mornings and her appetite seemed to have dwindled over the past few weeks.

Plus she had about two hundred dollars to her name. Things were tight, very tight.

"She'll also have some French toast with extra syrup," Colin added, "and some orange juice."

Lila scowled but made no comment until the waitress turned to walk away, her sneakers squeaking on the floor.

"What'd you do that for?" She turned to Colin, eager for an argument, anything to distract her from thinking about Clay.

He raised a brow and sat back against the seat. "You need to eat breakfast, Lila. You are not having just coffee."

"I think I'm old enough to decide for myself what I want for breakfast, Colin. You know I don't like eating in the mornings."

Trace sat back, crossing his arms as he watched them.

"We remember, but you seem to have forgotten Clay's rule about that," Colin said as the waitress brought over their coffee and milk.

Of course she hadn't forgotten. Clay had insisted that she eat something in the mornings, even if it was just an apple. He didn't want her going off for the day without something in her stomach.

She smiled as she remembered the quiet, patient way he'd spoken in his slow drawl. She eyed Colin and Trace. "I'm grown now. Those rules don't apply." Not that he'd had many—mostly things to do with respect and safety, like not staying out past curfew, and telling him where she was going, that sort of thing.

"Maybe not, but you've got to look after yourself," Trace said gently but firmly. "And we're going to ensure you do."

She didn't like the sound of that.

Colin squeezed her thigh, sending a shock of pleasure through her system and distracting her nicely. "I'm so glad to have you with us, you know. I missed you."

His words warmed her from the inside out and she melted, her annoyance at their high-handedness fading. "I missed you guys, too."

They both smiled at her and she realized it was true. They had missed her.

"So how's work going?" she asked Colin. "Clay said you were thinking about buying the vet practice from Sam Marshall."

"I did. Sam retired last month," Colin replied with a grin. "It's been busy, but good really good. Even if it means taking on Miss Angela and Elvis as my number one patients."

"Oh my God, is that dog still alive? He seemed ancient when I was a teenager."

Colin nodded with a smile. "Still alive. Of course, Miss Angela believes it's because he's the reincarnation of Elvis. I had to convince her last week that feeding him fried chicken was not good for him."

Lila giggled. "That dog would be more believable as Elvis reincarnated if he was a hound dog or something more masculine, but a Pomeranian?"

Trace kept silent as they talked, but then Trace had always been the quiet one. He was the only one of them who hadn't gone to college, preferring to work with horses than sit in a classroom.

Their plates of food arrived, the men's laden high with fried eggs, ham, potatoes and mushrooms. Her own plate had thick slices of French toast swimming in syrup.

"I can't eat all this," she said.

"Just do your best," Trace told her.

In the end she ate more than she thought she would. The three of them chatted easily; Trace and Colin catching her up on everything that had happened back home while she'd been away.

"Wow, I can't believe that Matt and Daisy got married," she said with a shake of her head. "I thought those two hated each other. Daisy was always playing mean tricks on Matt, and Matt was always threatening to blister her butt."

Colin snorted. "That girl has a devious mind."

"I seem to recall you helped her with quite a few of those pranks," Trace said.

Colin and Daisy had been in the same class and were good friends. Colin grinned. The waitress walked up, placing the bill on the table. Lila reached for her handbag, only to realize she'd left it in the truck.

"Damn."

"What's wrong, Lila?" Colin asked.

"I left my money in the truck. Could I have the keys?"

Both men simply stared at her. "You don't need any money," Colin said with a wink. "It's Trace's turn to pay."

Trace rolled his eyes, but stood and reached for his wallet.

"I can pay for mine," she protested.

Trace stilled and peered down at her. "Since when do you pay when you're out with us?"

She squirmed at the disapproval in his tone but then sighed and nodded. They were never going to let her pay when she was with them. As Trace paid at the counter, Colin leaned over to her. "How you doing, Lila? Feeling all right?"

She nodded. "I'm okay, just sad."

"We all are. Come on, let's get going; we should be home by dark."

He walked beside her, his hand on her lower back, guiding her, warming her insides. Each time he brushed against her, she felt her body react, heat pooling in the bottom of her stomach. Trace joined them outside as Colin helped her into the backseat. He opened the package he'd been carrying as she put her seatbelt on.

"Okay, Lila, open up for me."

"What?" she asked with a frown of confusion.

He held up a digital thermometer. "I want to check your temperature. I still don't like the sound of that cough or how pale you are."

"Colin, I'm fine. Honestly, compared to how I was last week I'm really healthy now."

Okay, that was probably the wrong thing to say. Colin scowled and held out the thermometer. Resigned to the fact that he wasn't going to change his mind, she gave in and opened her mouth.

When it beeped, he took it out and glanced down. "It's slightly high."

"Probably because I've just eaten," she suggested, unable to stop herself from coughing. He produced some cough syrup. She swallowed it down with a grimace.

"Just sit back and relax. We'll be home soon."

THE SUN WAS SETTING as they turned into the long driveway. Lila kept her eyes peeled, awaiting that first glimpse of the large, double-storied house with its wide porch. She remembered the first time she'd come here; she'd been absolutely terrified and too afraid to show it.

The awe she'd felt when she first saw the house hadn't diminished over the years. It still filled her with amazement that she got to live here. As they pulled up to the house, she felt a tug of happiness as she saw the silhouette of a large man standing at the top of the stairs, waiting for them.

They'd lied to her. Clay was okay.

"Seems like Gavin's eager to see you," Colin said with a chuckle.

Crushing disappointment stole her breath. Gavin. Of course. They hadn't lied. They wouldn't be that cruel. Not that she wasn't excited to see Gavin, but for a moment she'd hoped... She bit back a cry.

As the truck pulled to a stop, Gavin moved forward, coming around to her side. He opened her door, his gray eyes betraying his relief as he peered down at her intently. Lila's breath caught in her lungs as she stared up at him. His face hadn't changed much. He had a few more lines, a few gray hairs around his temple, which only added to his appeal. Gavin had a strong personality and his face reflected who he was—hard-working, dominant, masculine.

A smile curved his full lips. Damn, she had missed that smile.

"Hello, baby girl." Reaching across, he took her seatbelt off and she fell into his open arms with a small cry. He caught her easily, holding her against his massive chest.

She clung to his wide shoulders. He was even larger than she remembered but she knew he would never use his strength against her. Leaning down, he kissed her forehead, neither of them saying anything as they held onto each other tightly.

GAVIN CARRIED HIS SLIGHT, but infinitely precious bundle up the steps and into the house. He'd been waiting impatiently for his brothers to return with her. He'd wanted to go with them, but he'd been needed here. None of them liked to leave Clay alone at the moment; even though he was getting the best care money could buy.

This ranch had been in Clay's family for generations. Unfortunately, he was the last of the line. His sister had died when they were young and his other relatives were all distant cousins. When Clay had taken over the ranch from his father, it had been struggling. He'd turned it into a profitable business and Gavin was determined to carry on his legacy.

"I'm glad you're home, baby girl," he told Lila as he walked into the living room and sat on his recliner with her on his lap.

She stiffened and tried to hold herself upright, but he wasn't going to let her away with that. It was too long since he'd held her. He tugged her closer, resting his hand on her head as he ran his hand up and down her back

Lila coughed, wheezing slightly, and he frowned, glancing up at Colin and Trace with a question in his gaze.

"She's been sick," Colin explained, stretching. "I've been keeping an eye on her temperature. It's slightly high."

"We'll get her checked out in the morning then," Gavin decided. Nothing was as important as her health and well-being.

"*She* is right here," she said, struggling to sit up. This time he let her, wanting to see her face. She looked pale and tired, definitely thinner. He could see she needed some TLC and that's what he intended to lavish on her.

With some loving care and a few ground rules, they'd get her back to full health.

Gavin brushed the dark curls off her face. "Did you have a good trip?" He'd waited so long for her to come home, now that the moment was here it felt kind of surreal.

She nodded. "How's Clay?"

She looked so young. Was she old enough to handle what they wanted from her? Only twenty-three, still a baby, but then she'd always been more mature than her years.

"He's as good as can be expected, baby girl. If you're feeling all right tomorrow, I'll take you to see him."

"I'm fine," she insisted, ruining her protest with a cough.

"Hmm," he said, not committing to anything. "Well, why don't I run you a bath while we get your stuff in? Then you can have some dinner."

With a tired nod, Lila followed him upstairs. He filled the bath, while Trace and Colin brought her gear inside. Gavin looked at the two bags with a frown.

"You left some of her stuff there?" he asked his brothers as they met for a drink in the living room, leaving her to soak in the bathtub.

Trace shook his head with a sigh as he sat back in a plush armchair. Colin slouched on the couch, a beer in his hand.

"Nope," Colin said. "That was all she had. Well, she also had a mattress and an alarm clock but I figured we didn't need to bring them back with us."

"Her place came fully furnished then?" he asked. "She was always a bit of a tomboy but I figured she'd have more clothes than that."

Trace and Colin exchanged a look. "Well, if it was supposed to be furnished she got ripped off." As Colin explained where she'd been living, Gavin grew furious. He looked down at his clenched hands.

"So she was lying the entire time? To Clay?" Gavin knew for a fact that Clay wouldn't have let her live in such dire straits if he'd known. "I knew I should have gone and gotten her earlier."

"We couldn't; we promised Clay we'd wait," Colin reminded him.

"I know," Gavin sighed. "But it's been damn hard to stick to that promise and to think she's been living like... Damn it." He hit his fist against the arm of the chair.

"Yeah, well, we weren't too happy ourselves," Colin agreed. "No wonder she's been sick. Why do you think Clay didn't do something when he went to see her that last time?"

Gavin frowned and moved into the study. Coming back, he carried two envelopes. "Two different addresses," he said, looking at the letters Lila had written to Clay. "She must have moved. I bet he never saw the new apartment. Why would she move?"

"When we tried to question her about her job she wouldn't answer us," Trace mentioned.

Gavin looked over at him thoughtfully. "Think she lost it?"

"Maybe," Trace said. "This means she has no reason to return to Phoenix."

"She's here now," Gavin said with satisfaction. "And here is where she is going to stay."

3

Lila took a deep breath for courage before she walked into Clay's hospital room. She came to a sudden stop as she saw him lying on the bed, so still and surprisingly small. Clay had always been so large and healthy and just there. He was her rock.

She stepped forward quietly, not wanting to disturb him if he was sleeping. Gavin had driven her here and was now sitting out in the waiting room to give them some time alone. Clay's normally tanned skin was chalky and dark circles formed rings under his eyes. He'd lost so much weight that his cheeks were sunken and gaunt.

Tears welled in her eyes. Then he opened his eyes and looked up at her, his gaze filled with warmth, with Clay.

"Oh, Clay, I've missed you," she whispered, taking the seat beside the bed, her legs suddenly wobbly.

Clay held out his hand. "My little girl," he rasped. "Come lie with me."

"Are you sure?" she asked. "I don't want to hurt you."

"You could never hurt me, angel."

Lila climbed onto the bed, settling herself on her side, her head resting on his chest, same as she had when she was a small child and was feeling tired or scared or just in need of a cuddle.

"Why didn't you tell me?" she asked.

He ran a trembling hand up and down her back.

"I didn't want you being sad for too long. There was nothing anyone could do: there was no point in telling all of you."

Lila bit back her arguments. She didn't want to ruin their time with 'what ifs' or regrets.

"I love you, Clay." She held him as tight as she dared.

"I love you too, angel. Did I ever tell you that one of the best days of my life was the day you came into it? You brought sunshine into our home. I only wish you knew how much I adored having you around."

She patted his chest. "You're the most amazing person, Clay. You brought me home, gave me everything I could possibly need. I can never repay you."

"And you never have to. You're family, angel. Family doesn't owe family. Family is there for each other no matter what. You were mine from the moment I picked you up in that alley and you always will be."

Lila bit back her tears at his words.

"Shh, it's okay, angel. Just know that you were always mine. My daughter. Now, just let me hold you for a while. Are you okay? Have you been eating well? Taking care of yourself?"

Lila bit back a snort of laughter. Like father, like sons.

Gavin stepped into Clay's room. He waited forty minutes to give them some time to talk. A smile crossed his face as he saw them lying on the bed, Clay on his back, Lila on her side. They looked so peaceful.

Clay opened his eyes as Gavin stepped closer. "She's asleep. Poor thing is worn out." There was a question in his voice.

Knowing he couldn't hide much from Clay, Gavin sat beside the bed. "She's been sick. I had her at the doctor's this morning." With Lila protesting the whole time, not that he'd let that stop him. "She'll be okay as long as she gets plenty of rest and care." Which Gavin would make sure of. He had asked the doctor about bringing her to visit Clay here when she was still coughing. Although he knew how much Lila and Clay wanted to see each other, he didn't want to risk Clay catching something.

The doc, who knew Clay well, had smiled sadly and told him that seeing Lila would do Clay far more good than hurt.

Clay held her close as if afraid she would disappear. "It's good she's home. You and your brothers can take care of her now. I know I made you promise to let her be and perhaps that wasn't right of me to interfere. I just thought I was doing what was best."

Gavin nodded, staring at Lila lying so peacefully on the bed in full slumber. "I know. We all knew that you only ever wanted what was best for us."

Grasping his hand, Clay gave it a weak squeeze. "Don't scare her away and don't let her go. She needs to feel safe and loved. She needs to know she has a home."

"I know," Gavin agreed. "We'll take care of her."

They chatted for a while until Clay started to drift off.

"We should head home," Gavin said.

Clay nodded with regret, giving Lila a squeeze. "I don't want to let her go. Wake her up slowly. You know how she hates waking up suddenly."

Gavin smiled and walked around to where Lila lay. "You always were softer on her," he teased. "I remember you pouring a bottle of water on me one morning to force me out of bed."

Clay snorted. "Teenage boys, you'd have spent all day in bed if I let you. This one, she used to get up before all of us. I finally had to make a rule that she couldn't leave her room until I came to get her. At least until she got older. I was terrified she'd hurt herself after I caught her trying to cook us all breakfast. There she was, seven years old, standing on a step stool, frying eggs. She couldn't understand why I was so upset. She was just trying to do something nice. She thought she owed me for bringing her home. What she didn't understand was that every day was a blessing with her around."

Gavin knew how he felt. He ran a finger down her cheek. She murmured and rubbed her cheek with her hand.

"Baby girl, it's time to wake up now." He shook her gently. "Lila, its Gavin, you're safe." She sat up, gasping for breath and looking around in fright. Gavin's heart clenched, knowing this stemmed from a childhood of moving around constantly, of never knowing where she was going to wake up.

Clasping her face between his hands, he forced her to look at him. "You're in the hospital with me and Clay, Lila. You fell asleep."

"Oh, oh." She shook her head as though to clear it. "Clay." She glanced down at the older man, concern on her face. "I fell asleep, I'm sorry. Are you okay?"

"Of course, angel," Clay told her with a tired smile. "I'm just going to have a nap now."

She climbed down and Gavin moved back, but only slightly. "You go to sleep. I'll be here when you wake up."

Clay frowned. "I don't think so, angel."

"Lila, it's time we went home now," Gavin told her.

She glanced up at him. "I want to stay with Clay. I'll be quiet so he can rest. You can go home and pick me up later."

Gavin shook his head. "No can do, baby girl. You're coming home now." He made sure his voice held zero flexibility.

"Well, if you can't pick me up, I'm sure I can make my own way home."

He frowned. "Lila, have you forgotten you've been sick? You need to come home and get some rest."

"I can rest here," she replied stubbornly.

"Lila, honey," Clay spoke up before Gavin could. "Go home now. I'll still be here tomorrow. I promise."

She bit her lip, obviously wanting to argue, but then her shoulders slumped and she nodded, leaning over to kiss Clay on the forehead. "Sleep well. I love you."

"Love you too, angel."

CLAY DIED A WEEK LATER, surrounded by the family that loved him. Lila held it together through the arrangements, quietly organizing everything. They attended the small funeral together, leaning on one another and sharing family stories about the man they all loved with those who joined them at the house afterward.

"I thought Laken would have been here, supporting you," a deep voice commented as she stood at the sink, washing dishes. The crowd was thinning and she needed some time alone.

Sighing, she turned to look at Duncan Jones. The huge, darkly-tanned man had a slight scowl on his face. His black hair and dark eyes gave him an intense, serious look. And the fact that he was built like a tank had many people steering clear of him. Until they realized he was *the* Duncan Jones. Former pro-footballer and worth millions. Then they tended to swarm. She wondered if that was why he'd come back to Haven. Because here everyone treated him like they always had. As one of those Jones boys.

And there were quite a few of them.

"Well, hello to you, too, Duncan," she said dryly.

He had the grace to blush slightly and give her a sheepish smile. "Sorry, Lila, you know I'm not one to mince my words. Being one of ten boys meant that if you had something to say you'd better be quick and you'd better be loud. I'm sorry about Clay. I always had a lot of respect for him."

She smiled. "He liked you too. He always said, 'That Duncan Jones is going to make something of himself, despite his...'" she trailed off and it was her turn to blush.

"Despite my dead-beat, alcoholic father," Duncan finished with a raised brow.

"Ahh, I wouldn't quite say that," she said, heat filling her cheeks.

"It's okay, it's true." He smiled wryly.

"Laken wanted to be here." She tried to change the subject back to something safer. "But she had other things going on." Lila was concerned about her best friend. She'd met Laken Philips her first day of school here in Haven. The other girl had pulled her hair and they'd become instant enemies.

That had lasted a week until Lila caught some older boys teasing Laken, and jumped in to defend her. They'd been best friends ever since. Laken had moved to New York to pursue a career in fashion. But lately she'd sounded tired and sad whenever Lila spoke to her.

Duncan frowned. "They're working her too hard, taking advantage of her."

Lila raised her brows but refrained from asking Duncan how Laken was any of his business. As far as she knew the two of them were like oil and water together.

"Hey, Duncan, you ready to go?" Joe, one of Duncan's younger brothers, came up to them and after talking politely with Lila for a few minutes the two of them left.

"Lila, honey," a deep voice called out to her. Lila looked up, having to smile as an extremely tall man with thick white hair walked towards her. His wife walked beside him, holding his hand. She was the complete opposite of her husband, round and very short.

"Mr. and Mrs. Atchison, thank you for everything you've done today," she said warmly. Arch Atchison was the undertaker; his wife, Mina, worked as his assistant. Being that there weren't that many deaths in Haven, Arch also worked as the town's postman and he did a comedy night once a month at the local bar, Dirty Delights. Amazing how funny an undertaker could be.

"You're welcome dear," Mina told her with a smile. She patted Lila's hands as she held them tightly. "Anything we can do to help, just let me know."

"I will, thank you."

They left and she turned back to her dishes.

"Hard to get a moment alone, isn't it?" A familiar deep voice said behind her before two hands landed on her shoulders.

"Jake," she said, turning with a smile as she launched herself into the Sheriff's arms. Although he was nearly ten years older than she was, Lila knew him well. He'd been Gavin's best friend for years and she'd had a bit of a crush on him as a teenager.

"How you holding up, kid?" he asked. "Want me to get rid of everyone for you?"

She pulled back, but he kept hold of her shoulders. "What are you going to do? Arrest them?"

"For you, baby, anything."

She giggled.

"How about you take your hands off her," Gavin interjected. Lila looked over, surprised to see him scowling at them. She wondered what his problem was as Jake laughed and took a step back, holding up his hands.

"Calm down, my friend. I was just leaving."

"I'll see you out," Gavin told him coldly.

Lila watched them walk out, then shook her head and went back to her dishes. Men. They were a mystery to her.

An hour later everyone had finally gone. Feeling utterly drained, Lila looked around for something else to do, anything to keep her mind off the fact that Clay was gone. She couldn't sit still, couldn't stop, or she feared she'd never start moving again.

Lila moved onto the porch and looked out over the land Clay had loved. Her heart broke that he'd never see it again, never ride across it, never again sit on his porch and drink a beer. Tears dripped down her cheeks and suddenly it was too much. She'd held it all inside for days and now it was erupting out of her.

She took off, racing to her favorite black cherry tree. There, she collapsed on the ground with a scream, bashing her fists against the ground.

"Why, why, why, why!" she screamed. "Why'd you leave me?"

She loved him so much and it was tearing her apart to have lost him. Why hadn't she spent more time with him, visited more often, called him, anything?

Warm arms surrounded her and the world tilted dizzily. Tears blurred everything around her, but she made out Gavin's face. He sat on the ground with her on his lap, rocking her as she cried.

Finally spent, exhausted, she just lay there, resting against him as he kissed the top of her head.

"Good girl. About time you let it all out. You've been so brave for the rest of us, it's time to let us look after you."

Lila wiped her face as footsteps came towards them.

"Here, Lila." Colin held out some tissues to her. She wiped her eyes and blew her nose, feeling a lot better. Trace handed her a glass of water and she sipped it, starting to feel half alive.

"Sorry," she muttered, her cheeks flooding with heat as she realized she'd totally broken down on them.

"For what?" Colin sat beside them so he could reach over and grab one of her hands. She felt Trace scoot up behind her. It was a heady feeling, having them surround her like this. A dream come true, but one that would forever remain a fantasy.

"For breaking down like this, I'm not the only one grieving. It was selfish." She tried to move off Gavin's lap. But his arms remained steady, not squeezing her, but letting her know that she wasn't going anywhere until he was ready for her to.

"It was about time you let it all out, sweetheart," Colin told her. "You've been holding your emotions inside, staying strong for the rest of us. It's time to lean on us for a change."

"For a change?" she snorted. "I've been leaning on you guys since I got here. You haven't let me contribute to the household finances. You've barely let me lift a finger. It was my turn to do something for you."

They went still, silent, and she bit her lip, confused by their furious expressions. Had she said something wrong?

She pulled at Gavin's arms. "Let me go, Gavin. I've got to go pack."

"Pack?" Gavin frowned. "Where do you think you're going?"

"Gavin, let me up," she demanded. Finally, he loosened his hold. As she stood they did as well. With other men she might have felt intimidated as they surrounded her, but she knew they would never hurt her. They'd harm themselves before hurting her. That was just the kind of men they were. Men who had honor, who would always protect those weaker than they were.

"Well?" Colin asked. "Where are you planning on going?"

"I need to get back to my apartment before my landlord rents it out to someone else." *If he hasn't already.*

"Your apartment is long gone," Gavin told her with a piercing look. "We broke your lease and paid the fees. Did you really think we would let you go back there?"

"You did what?" Her temper stirred.

"That place was dangerous, Lila," Trace added gently, as always trying to be the voice of reason. "It was unsafe and unhealthy. You weren't taking care of yourself. You need to stay here where we can look after you."

"But you don't want me here!"

Trace frowned. "Of course we do. This is your home. Here,

people love you and want what's best for you. I can't understand why you would want to leave."

"Because none of you want me! You never wanted me and now that Clay's dead there is no reason for me to be here!"

She tried to slip between Gavin and Colin, but Gavin grabbed her, holding her in place.

"Sweetheart, what are you talking about?" Colin asked with concern. "What do you mean we don't want you here?"

"I know it's true, Colin." She stared up into his deep brown eyes. "You don't have to pretend otherwise. You guys only put up with me because of Clay. I'll get out of your way now and you won't have to worry about me anymore."

"My God, girl, if you don't start making sense I'm going to put you over my knee and spank you until I get a straight answer. What the hell makes you think we don't want you here?" Gavin roared. The other two looked equally furious.

"I know you only put up with me because of Clay; I've known from the start, when I overheard Trace and Colin."

Trace and Colin looked at each other in surprise. "Heard us say what, Lila?" Colin asked.

She wrenched her arm free from Gavin's hold. "Soon after I got here, I overheard the two of you talking. Both of you agreed that you didn't want me here, that I would just get in the way and ruin everything. Colin was mad because I was taking up all of Clay's time and Trace figured I'd just get in the way and that I'd ruin all your fun. I heard Trace say that if Clay had to pick up a stray at least it could have been a boy and Colin agreed and said I was such a baby I'd probably whine all the time and act like a brat."

"Jesus Christ... Oh, Lila." Colin reached out to touch her, but she shied back into Gavin.

"So I tried my hardest to fit in with all of you, to not whine or act up or cause any trouble because I knew that one word from you guys and Clay would send me back."

She looked away, totally done for. This last week had been an emotional roller-coaster and she was exhausted and so very sad. Not only had she lost Clay but she'd lost the three men she loved as well. Not that she'd ever really had them.

"Lila, what you heard were two teenage brats mouthing off," Trace told her desperately. "We didn't mean it. God, we were just two selfish kids who didn't like change. Within a week after that we both loved you. We would never have sent you away. Hell, I can't believe you heard that. Clay would have kicked our asses if he knew. Honey, he would never, ever have sent you away. You were his daughter."

Lila knew deep down that he spoke the truth. She knew they'd just been kids mouthing off. But that little seven-year-old hadn't known and she'd had a childhood of being disposable. She didn't want to lose the best thing she'd ever had.

"Damn straight Clay would have kicked your asses." Gavin's voice was quiet, so cold and angry that she shivered. "Damn it. I can't believe you thought we would get rid of you. Fuck!"

She let out a deep breath. "It wasn't Colin and Trace's fault that I never truly believed that Clay wanted me—it was mine. It was my shitty childhood. I could have reached out, could have talked to Clay about this, but I didn't. Then when I went to college, the three of you all acted like I didn't even exist. All of you refused to take me fishing, riding or anywhere and when I decided to move to Phoenix, you all helped me pack."

Gavin stepped forward, leaning over her. "Oh, we wanted you here, baby. Ain't no two ways about that. But we made a promise to Clay to let you experience life away from here before we claimed you. Yeah, we acted like jerks for a while there and I am truly sorry for the hurt and confusion we caused. The reason we tried to keep some distance is because we all knew if we let you close, we'd have you in our bed faster than a jackrabbit on moonshine. So while we didn't want you to go, we knew we had to let you or you'd have been ours."

Ours?

"Uhh, what do you mean *ours*?" she asked nervously as Trace and Colin moved in close behind her.

"We, as in the three of us," Gavin told her. "We want you, Lila. We have for a long time. In our bed, in our lives, as our wife."

Leaning down, Gavin kissed her and fireworks exploded. He pulled back and Trace turned her, taking her into his arms. His kiss was gentler but no less intense. By the time Colin got to her, her head was spinning and she was floating, as though she were on drugs.

Then the world really did shift and turn as Gavin grabbed her, slinging her over his shoulder.

"Hey, wait, what are you doing?" she cried out, wiggling to try to get free.

Smack!

She stilled as a heavy hand landed on her buttocks. Did he seriously just spank her?

"Be still, Lila," he told her. "We're going inside to have a talk."

"Did you just hit me?" she squealed.

Gavin snorted. "That? That was just a little smack to get your attention. Calm down."

My God, he only seemed to get bossier as he got older.

"I should really clean up the rest of the house first, don't you think?" she said, desperately looking to put off this little chat. She needed to think through what they'd said. They couldn't seriously want her, could they?

And yet, they didn't lie. Not once could she remember them telling a mistruth.

"You're not lifting another finger," he informed her. "You've done enough already. There's hardly anything left to do. We'll do the rest. After we talk."

"I don't know if I want to talk."

"Baby, we need to talk and we can't put it off just because you're scared."

The world swirled around her once more as he placed her gently on the sofa in the living room. She immediately shot to her feet. Gavin softly pushed her back down.

"Let me up," she said, fighting against his hold.

"Sit down, Lila." His voice was quiet, but infused with pure, unbendable steel.

"No."

"Lila, calm down; I don't want you hurting yourself."

He gathered her up into his arms and sat with her on the couch.

"God, baby, don't ever threaten to leave again. Please," he begged her, his voice breaking. She was amazed by that. Gavin was always so strong, so invincible. He didn't hesitate or falter. And yet he sounded terrified at the idea of her leaving. Suddenly, she wanted to be the one comforting him. "I don't think my heart could stand it."

A hand touched hers and she looked up to see Trace sitting beside them. Turning her head she saw Colin perched on the coffee table, looking at her in concern.

"Please stay with us. Nothing needs to happen," Colin said sadly, his eyes filled with such pain that she immediately reached for him. "We won't force you into anything. But no matter what, you will always be a part of this family. The last thing we want is for you to not feel welcome in your own home."

Gavin squeezed her hand. "I wish now that you had acted up as a child. Then you would know that Clay would never have kicked you out of our lives, no matter what. You were such a perfect child. I never saw it for what it really was—a fear of being rejected. Honey, if you'd done something naughty, Clay would have just punished you, then forgiven you. You might have ended up with a sore butt but he would never have rejected you. You were his daughter."

She sniffled, wanting desperately to believe them. But it was so hard to turn around beliefs she'd held for years.

"He never spanked me. Well, once, when he caught me cooking on the grill. He gave me a couple of pats on the butt, but they didn't really hurt."

"He told me about that," Gavin admitted. "He was afraid you'd hurt yourself. You scared him."

"I did?"

Gavin nodded. "You were so fearless, so independent. I found myself wishing you'd rely on us a bit more. I can remember once when I saw you running towards the barn to Clay. You missed seeing a hole in the ground and came crashing down.

"I came racing towards you, totally expecting you to start screaming. But you just stood up and brushed your hands off. When you looked up at me, I could see the tears in your eyes. But you just told me that you were all right. I wanted to take you into my arms and give you a hug, but you were acting so brave, I didn't think you'd appreciate it." He ran his hand over her hair.

"Wasn't until later that day when you were in your bathing suit that Clay saw how bruised you were. Any other eight-year-old would have been crying and wanting reassurance but not our little miss independent. So tough."

She shook her head. "Not really. Most of the time I was terrified but I didn't want to let any of you down."

"God." Trace ran his hand over his face. "And in the end, we all let you down. You thought you weren't loved when we have loved you forever."

She bit at her lip, staring at them all. "I-I love you guys, too. It was part of the reason I had to leave. I never imagined that one of you would want me. Let alone the three of you. I couldn't stay here and watch you guys meet other women."

"We don't want anyone but you," Gavin growled. "We haven't for years. Stay here with us, be with us. Let us show you how much we love you."

"This all feels like a dream," she said. "Are you sure it's what you really want? Are you sure we can make it work?"

Gavin ran his hand up and down her back. "We've known for years we wanted to share the same woman. We're closer than brothers, baby girl, we have a bond that goes beyond that. We know that it will take work. But we will make it work. And you are the one woman for us."

Tears welled in her eyes. "I want to believe, I do. It's just..."

"You're scared to trust. Scared to believe. And we're to blame for that," Colin said bitterly, anger and pain filling his eyes.

"Well, the only way you're going to believe us is if we earn your trust," Gavin said. "And to do that, you need to stay here. You need to learn that no matter what happens we are here for you. With a lot of love and support we'll show you that you're meant to be with us."

"What if things don't work out? What if you come to hate me?" The last thing she wanted was to lose them forever.

They wrapped her up within the three of them, surrounding her.

"Nothing in life is guaranteed, Lila," Gavin said. "We could go on as we are and never take a risk. But would any of us ever be truly happy? What the four of us could have together is worth the risk. We've been miserable without you. We're all willing to do whatever is needed to make you happy."

With a sigh, she fell back against Gavin's chest. They were her fantasy and it wasn't every day that she had the opportunity to make her fantasies come true.

"Please, Lila, we know this is a lot to take in," Trace said. "We realize we're not the easiest guys in the world to get along with. Just say you'll stay for a while. We can take things as slow as you want. You're our whole world and we will do anything to keep you. We'd even try to change if that's what you needed. Make ourselves more metro."

She burst into laughter. "Metro? Do you even know what that means? No, I don't think you guys could ever pull off metro and I don't want you to change who you are. Then you wouldn't be you."

Another giggle escaped her.

"What?" Gavin asked.

"Just thinking of you using gel to style your hair, and getting a pedicure."

"Oh, that's funny, is it?" Gavin mock-growled as he tickled her.

She roared with laughter. "No, Gavin. Stop! Stop! You're going to make me pee!"

"Well, what do I get if I stop?" he teased.

"A kiss! A kiss!" she yelled.

Immediately he stopped. "Well, all right then." He leaned back and she caught her breath, staring at his lush lips. She licked her own, feeling her skin go red, her nipples press against her bra.

Leaning in, she took his mouth with hers. Damn, he tasted good. His scent surrounded her, spurring her on. She placed her hands around his neck, pushing her breasts against his chest, trying to find some friction.

"That is so hot," Trace moaned, bringing her back into the now. She leaned back, breathing heavily.

Gavin ran his hand up her thigh, until he came close to reaching her pussy. Wow, she wanted him, all three of them. But as much as she desired them, she didn't want to immediately jump into bed with them.

Because she knew once she went to bed with them, everything else was going to take a backseat and she wanted to build a relationship with them that would last.

She'd only slept with two men in her life and neither of those experiences had been all that marvellous. Truthfully, she was really intimidated by the idea of sleeping with them. She knew they were far more experienced than she was.

Gavin's touch grew bolder, eating away at her self-control. She gritted her teeth and forced herself to pull his hand from her leg.

He looked at her in surprise.

"I can't sleep with you," she blurted out. All three men went silent and turned to look at her, their gazes shocked. "Yet. I can't sleep with you yet. Don't get me wrong, I want to. Dear Lord, how I want to," she muttered, rubbing her thighs together to try and ease the ache in her pussy. "But being with the three of you, it's so much to take in, and I just...sex will just...when we have sex, I want to feel secure in us."

They were silent for a long moment and she wondered if she'd ruined everything. Then Gavin nodded and Trace smiled. Surprisingly, it was Colin who looked serious.

"I understand, baby girl," Gavin said, drawing her attention away from Colin. "I even agree that it's a good idea."

She flung her arms around his neck, holding him tight. "Thank you."

"Whatever you need, baby girl, we only want what's best for you," he told her.

Sitting back, she took in a deep breath. "I know it's going to be hard, on all of us."

"You know what they say," Colin said with a sigh. "Love hurts."

Trace elbowed him. "I don't think they were talking about a hard-on, idiot."

"Hey, you don't know that," Colin protested. She was glad to see him smiling once more. "But staying means agreeing to a relationship with all of us—and that includes accepting our discipline. We can't change this part of ourselves, because we want nothing more than to keep you safe and healthy."

"Couldn't you just scold me?" she asked.

Gavin grinned. "Afraid not, baby girl, spankings work far better."

"You know that as well as we do, Lila," Trace pointed out, sounding far too reasonable. "Have you seen happier women than those who live in Haven?"

The women of Haven certainly weren't downtrodden or submissive. They were some of the happiest, most content women she'd ever met.

She shook her head. No, she hadn't. And truthfully, her protests were more for show than anything else. The idea of a spanking was kind of intriguing.

"I love you guys so much. I want nothing more than to see where this goes. I'll stay. But if things don't work out, if I decide I need to leave, then you have to let me go."

The three of them stared at her before breaking into wide grins.

"You won't regret this, Lila. I promise," Colin swore to her as they all gathered for one long, glorious embrace.

She hoped not. She really did.

4

————————

Gavin walked down the stairs. Lila was resting, obviously exhausted. This last week had taken a lot out of all of them.

He stilled as he came to the bottom of the steps and remembered what today had been all about. Clay was gone. His foster father had molded him into the man he was today and he would never forget him. He'd taken a lost, sullen teenage boy in and turned his life around.

"I love you," he whispered, before continuing on to the kitchen where Colin and Trace were cleaning up the last of the mess.

"Lila resting?" Trace asked as he tidied up the large room.

"Yeah," Gavin said tiredly. "She's tuckered out. God, imagine thinking all these years that if she did something wrong she'd be kicked out."

"It's our fault," Colin said, his eyes stricken. "I can't believe she overheard us."

Trace shook his head, his face filled with guilt. "We deserve to be horsewhipped."

Gavin sighed and sat at the table. "You were kids, you didn't mean it. You have to let it go. Holding onto the guilt isn't helping anyone, least of all Lila. What we do from now on is what counts. We have to make sure that she knows how much we love her. That she feels secure enough to be herself."

"Today is the closest I've ever seen her throw a temper tantrum," Trace mused.

"Exactly," Gavin replied. "And how weird is that when we've known her since she was seven? She was always so good. Too good. The more she acts out, the safer she feels."

"So we can expect a brat, huh?" Colin asked his face pensive. Gavin worried over how his youngest brother would handle this. He'd been hurt badly in the past and Gavin knew he still carried scars. He just hoped that Colin didn't end up tarring this relationship with his past pain.

"Maybe. We need to stick together and show her that this can work. She still has her doubts and she's going to have them until she learns that she is the most important thing in the world to us and we will never let her go." Gavin intended to ensure that Lila was as safe as he could make her.

LILA SAT at the kitchen table the next morning and stifled a yawn. She'd lain awake last night thinking about the last week.

She'd cried a few times as she'd remembered Clay. She'd even dreamed about him. It had felt so real. In her dream he'd hugged her and told her he was proud of her. Then he'd said that sometimes it was harder to go for what your heart really desired. But if she took that plunge she'd find happiness far beyond what she could have imagined.

"Do you need to call and quit your job?" Gavin asked her suddenly.

She glanced up at the three men sitting around the table. "Ahh, no." They stared at her quizzically and she realized she had to give them more than that. "I lost it."

Trace squeezed her hand in sympathy. "Cutbacks?" he asked.

She nodded, feeling embarrassed. Even though it hadn't been through any fault of her own, she still felt ashamed that she'd lost her job. But she'd been the newest employee at the museum; it made sense that they would let her go first.

Gavin leaned back in his chair, watching her intently. She blushed under his perusal, her nipples stiffening beneath her loose t-shirt. Her need for them was growing with every minute.

She couldn't stop imagining the three of them touching her, teasing her. Why had she made that no sex rule?

Lila licked her lips, staring over at Trace hungrily.

"Sweetheart, you keep staring at me like that and I won't be able to control myself," he told her huskily.

"Maybe you shouldn't," she replied. "Control yourself, that is. I'm starting to think I was a bit hasty about the whole no sex thing."

Her men drew their breath in sharply, staring at her as her pussy clenched fiercely.

Gavin shook his head. "Ahh, baby, you don't know how much I long to just pick you up, take you upstairs and keep you in bed for the next week or two. But, and I can't believe I'm saying this, you were right to insist we take this slow. When we make love to you we will claim you and there will be no going back. So you need to be very sure. And I'm not sure you're there yet."

Damn him, why couldn't he be just a normal man and jump at the chance of sex? She grinned wryly. "You're right. But it's so hard not to touch you guys."

"No one said you couldn't touch us," Colin replied. "Just be gentle." He reached down with a pained look to adjust himself. "What are you planning on doing today?"

"I think I'll go for a ride," she replied. She pushed her eggs around on her plate, not really feeling hungry.

"I don't think so," Gavin said as he finished off a huge plate of ham, eggs and potatoes. Gavin was an amazing cook, but Colin was the breakfast king.

"Why not?" she asked with a puzzled frown. She'd been for a few rides since she'd been back, riding her old horse, Sunshine. Clay had bought her Sunshine on her twelfth birthday. The boys nearly had a fit when they'd seen the size of him. Lila had fallen instantly in love with the grumpy horse. Sure, the stallion was far bigger than she was, but she was the more stubborn of the two. And she soon won the horse over.

It had taken a while for the guys to relax, though. Now that she thought about it, one of them had constantly followed her around every time she went for a ride for the first month. At the time she'd been annoyed, believing they didn't think she was good enough to ride Sunshine. Now she realized they'd simply been scared.

"Because you're all tuckered out," Gavin told her, running his hand over her head.

Colin brushed his thumbs under her eyes. "You have dark circles under your eyes. Didn't you sleep last night?"

She shrugged. "Not really. I kept having funny dreams."

"Want to talk about them?" Trace asked with concern as he rose to place his plate in the dishwasher.

Lila shook her head. She just wasn't comfortable sharing some things yet.

"I want you to get some rest today, baby," Gavin told her.

"I'll rest this afternoon. After I get back from my ride," she said firmly, ignoring the three frowning faces that stared back at her. She wasn't about to let them just take over her life and they needed to realize that.

"All right, but be back by lunch," Gavin bossed. "Make sure

you take some water with you as well, it's a hot day out there and you'll dehydrate. And take your phone."

They'd been horrified that she'd lost her phone. Not that she'd been able to afford to keep paying for it, anyway. Gavin had gone out and bought her a new phone and, despite her protests, was paying the bill for it. She really needed to get a job. Especially if she was staying.

Lila barely refrained from rolling her eyes, but she couldn't help the mocking salute. "Sir, yes, Sir."

Gavin narrowed his eyes but she saw his lips twitched. "When did you become such a smart ass?"

"I learned it all from Colin," she answered quickly.

Colin leaned back, holding his hands up in a placating gesture, although his eyes danced with amusement. "Hey, I have no idea what she's talking about."

Gavin just shook his head as he got up and placed his plate in the sink.

"Is there something wrong with your food?" Colin asked.

"Oh, no, sorry. It's very nice. I'm just not hungry."

"You need to eat something before you ride out, honey," Trace said, kissing her on the forehead. As she raised her face up, he took her lips. Gently at first then he slipped his tongue in, teasing her, tasting her.

When he pulled back, she was dazed, shivering with excitement.

"Eat something. I'll see you at lunch." With a final caress of her shoulder, he left.

Gavin moved over to her and, lifting her to her feet, cuddled her close before leaning down to brush her lips with his, once, twice until she'd had enough of his teasing. Placing her hands behind his neck, something she could only do because he was already bent over, she pulled him down, kissing him soundly.

They separated and he chuckled. "Be good. Remember what I

told you and I'll see you at lunch." With a pat to her bottom—did the man have an ass fixation or what? —he left.

"Are you all hanging around today?" she asked Colin as he cleared up the rest of breakfast. He was a bit of a neat freak. Unlike Gavin who made a hell of a mess, Colin liked to clean as he cooked.

"Nah, just Trace and Gavin. I've got to go do some rounds. I'll be back early tonight." Then he tugged her close and smacked her lips with his, running his hand up and down her back. "Behave. Eat something."

Suddenly she had the house to herself and it was far too quiet. Yeah, a ride was exactly what she needed. Dumping her breakfast, she turned the dishwasher on before climbing the stairs to her room. Pulling on some stretch pants and a tank-top, she slathered on sunscreen and grabbed her phone, putting it in her back pocket.

Moving downstairs, she grabbed a bottle of water from the fridge and a small backpack from the hall cupboard. Sipping on the water, she moved out to the stables.

"Hey, Lila," Ron greeted her. He was one of their older ranch hands; he'd been around as long as she could remember.

"Hey, Ron," she called back.

"You taking Sunshine out?" he asked, coming towards her.

"Yep, thought I'd go for a short ride."

Ron nodded. "I'll saddle him for you." He moved away before she could protest that she could take care of the task herself.

She was placing her water bottle and cell phone in her backpack when her phone beeped. Smiling as she saw Laken's name on the display, she read the text then quickly shot off a reply.

Ron brought Sunshine out, distracting her. She placed her backpack down, resting her phone on a fence post as she patted Sunshine, crooning to him. He ate up the attention.

"Just a big baby. Except when it comes to riding him, then he's strictly a one-woman horse," Ron teased. "I'll see you later, kid. Ride safely. Which direction you headed in?"

"Thought I'd head towards the lake. Sunshine and I like sitting by that old shack."

He snorted. "Old shack, more like a few planks of wood held together by two rusty nails."

"That's the one." She grinned.

ABOUT AN HOUR LATER, Lila pulled Sunshine to a stop and let out a long sigh. This had always been her thinking spot. Clay had known about it but he'd never told the boys, although she wouldn't be surprised if they knew.

Tethering Sunshine in the shade, she moved over to sit and look at the lake, drawing her bottle of water out. Taking a long drink, she wiped her forehead. It was a scorcher today. She'd taken the ride slowly, just enjoying the day.

Lying back, her mind immediately turned to her men. Her men. God, part of her still thought she was dreaming. She couldn't believe that they returned her feelings.

Part of her wondered if it could last.

She'd never really believed in forever. Things always came to an end. Her father had abandoned her. Her mother had given her away.

The only person to keep her was Clay and now even he had left her.

How the hell could she trust them to stick around?

You need to try.

The thought whispered through her head, but the voice sounded suspiciously like Clay's. She didn't believe in ghosts, but she figured if she would ever have a guardian angel it would be Clay.

This was right. She knew it was. They were going to be hers.

"Jeez Louise." She rubbed her eyes, yawning tiredly. "Maybe just a little nap and then I'll head back."

Closing her eyes, she drifted off.

GAVIN STOOD in the kitchen peering out the window with a frown. He glanced over at the clock. 1pm. She should have been back by now. He'd already made sandwiches for lunch.

Picking up his phone, he tried calling her. It rang then went to voicemail.

Where the hell was she? He'd give her another ten minutes then he was going looking for her and God help her when he found her.

Trace walked into the kitchen. "Lila's still not home?"

Gavin shook his head and grabbed up his phone. "I'm going to head out and look for her. She should have been home an hour ago."

"Think she lost track of time?" Trace asked, following him out.

"I don't know, but she's not answering her phone."

Gavin tried calling her again as he walked. He came to a stop as he heard a ring tone. Trace followed the sound over to a wooden post, picking up the silver phone that Gavin had bought her a few days ago. Two days and she'd already managed to misplace it.

"God damn it, that girl is in trouble when I catch up with her," he muttered.

"Gavin, Trace," Ron called out in greeting.

"Hey, Ron, you haven't seen Lila, have you?" Trace asked.

Ron frowned. "Not since I saddled Sunshine for her this morning. I thought she'd be back by now."

"So did we," Gavin said grimly. "Don't know what direction she went in do you?" Looking for her was going to be like searching out a needle in a haystack.

"I can do you one better, I know where she went," Ron said, surprising him. "She said she was headed for the lake, by that wreck of a shack."

Her thinking spot. They all knew about it and had always given her privacy when she went there.

"I'll come with you," Trace said quickly. "I'll just run back and get some water."

Worry churning in his gut, his instincts screaming at him to find her quick, Gavin saddled up his horse, while Ron did the same for Trace's big beast.

LILA RUBBED HER EYES TIREDLY, wondering why every bone in her body ached. When had her mattress grown so hard? Rolling over, she opened her eyes slightly. She must have forgotten to pull her drapes shut. Weird.

Forcing herself to fully wake up, she looked around, confused and a bit frightened.

"What the hell?" She must have fallen asleep outside. "Oh shit." Frantically, she raised her wrist up to her still-blurry eyes, barely making out the hands on her watch face.

1:45pm. Oh, she was in so much trouble.

Hastily, she stood, her body swaying. Black circled her vision as her stomach protested the movement.

The world around her swirled sickeningly and suddenly the ground came up to meet her as she fainted dead away.

"LILA!" Trace yelled as he saw her stand then immediately drop to the ground. He forced his horse to go faster. Gavin did the same but his horse didn't have the speed Trace's did. Trace reached her first, jumping off his horse to run to where she lay so quiet and still.

"Oh God, honey, please be all right," he begged as he frantically ran his hands over her, looking for injuries. They'd just gotten her back, she couldn't leave them now. He only felt whole when Lila was around.

"What's wrong with her?" Gavin barked as he came to his knees beside them, his hands joining Trace's.

Trace felt his brother's pain, knew he was just as terrified as Trace was. Gavin had led a hard life before Clay had brought him home. He'd been big for his age and older kids had constantly picked fights with him just to prove they could beat him.

Gavin had grown up fighting. Where Trace and Colin had only experienced one foster home, he'd been in and out of them since the age of eight when his father had been sent off to jail.

Gavin didn't open up easily to people. But for some reason he'd taken two terrified younger boys under his wing. He'd protected them from the bullies who would have had a field day with two middle-class boys who were used to the loving protection of their parents.

And Trace, who'd done his best to look after his younger brother, had been forever grateful. He'd been just as scared as Colin, but tried to hold it together for his brother's sake.

When Clay had come for them, Trace knew he couldn't leave without Gavin. The smart-mouthed fifteen-year-old had put on a brave face, but Trace knew that Gavin cared about them. Even loved them in a gruff, teenage boy, way. And so Trace had marched up to Clay, who'd been loading their stuff into his huge-ass black truck, and with his voice cracking, he'd told Clay that he wasn't leaving unless Gavin came with them.

Clay had turned slowly and looked at him, before glancing over his shoulder at where Gavin was saying good-bye to Colin.

"That so?" he'd drawled.

Trace had nodded, swallowing heavily to disguise his nerves. "Yes, sir. Please?" he'd added, losing his bravado as Clay had continued to stare at him. He had only met his godfather a handful of times and he was kind of intimidated by the big man.

Clay hadn't said a thing, just walked past Trace up to Gavin who'd stared at the larger man, his shoulders back. Clay was taller than Gavin by a few inches and with far more muscle, but Trace knew Gavin would take him on if he had to.

"Are you, Gavin?" Clay asked, coming to a stop, staring at the boy.

"Yes," Gavin replied. "You're their godfather?"

Clay nodded.

"Took you long enough to get here," Gavin told him. Trace sucked in a breath, certain Clay would hit back, but he just stood there calmly. "They don't belong here. They're easy pickings."

"Really? They seem in okay shape."

"Because Gavin looked after us," Colin had told him bravely. Both Gavin and Trace had glared at him to keep him quiet, Gavin even tugging the smaller boy behind him.

Clay raised a brow. "That so? And you?" he'd asked Gavin. "Do you belong here?"

Gavin shrugged. "Not like anyone wants me."

Clay had nodded and turned. Disappointment almost made Trace sick. Then the big man had called back over his shoulder, "Grab your stuff, Gavin."

"What?" Gavin asked.

"You're coming home with us. I need to call the social worker. Damn, I hate paperwork."

"Why?" Gavin had asked.

Clay turned, looking at him. "Because I want you. Now get moving."

Trace looked over at present-day Gavin. He'd always kept a

part of himself separate from everyone but his family, he didn't let others close. But Trace knew that Lila was the one person that could bring the big guy to his knees.

"Do you think she hit her head?" Gavin asked Trace, looking up at him.

Trace stared down at Lila. She was pale, too pale. "I don't know. There's no blood. She seemed to just faint."

A low groan came from Lila as she tried to move. They held her still as she opened her eyes, peering up at them. Trace let out a low sigh.

"Trace? Gavin?" she asked groggily. "What are you guys doing in my room?"

Trace ran his hand over her head as Gavin took her pulse. He felt sick with relief. Damn, she'd scared him. She was so tiny, so delicate that at times it terrified him. Especially when she was ill or hurt.

He brushed back her dark curls, wishing her smooth skin held more color.

"We're not in your room, honey," he told her. "We're by the lake, you fainted."

Was she ill? Was there something seriously wrong with her? Worry made him almost light-headed as he continued to run his hand over her silken hair. First his parents had died, then Clay, he wasn't about to let anything happen to the most important person in his life. Even if that meant wrapping her in cotton wool and locking her in her bedroom until she was eighty.

He smiled slightly at the thought. He could just imagine her reaction if he tried to do just that. Their kitten had claws when she was riled.

"I did?" she asked with surprise. "I've never fainted before." She frowned. "I fell asleep. When I woke up I saw the time and realized I was running really late. I must have stood up too quickly or something."

She moved, attempting to sit up. Trace and Gavin reached for her at the same time, holding her down.

"Just where do you think you're going?" Gavin barked. The more worried he grew, the gruffer he got. Most people thought him bad-tempered and gave him a wide berth, something that didn't bother Gavin in the slightest. But when someone he loved was at risk Gavin could be like a bear with a sore paw.

"Just lay still, honey," Trace added soothingly. "We don't want you fainting again."

"Probably a combination of too much sun and too little food," Gavin commented, frowning at her. "When we get you home, you're going straight to bed, little girl."

Lila heaved a big sigh. Trace's gaze was drawn to her chest as her breasts rose and fell. She had a slim build, yet, she had curves in all the right places. He remembered the last time he saw her in a bathing suit, a tiny little bikini she'd worn around the summer she turned nineteen.

Oh yeah, he remembered that well. When he'd first realised she was a woman and not a little girl anymore. After that he'd learned to stay away when she was out by the pool.

"I'm fine, Gavin. I am sorry I worried you guys. You didn't need to come looking for me, I know how busy you both are."

Trace stared at her incredulously. Did she think they'd just eat their lunch then go back to work?

She chewed on her lower lip. "I've probably put you way behind in your work. I can make my own way home now."

"Do you seriously think we'd just leave you here after you fainted and go off to work as though there was nothing wrong?" Trace asked. Gavin, it seemed, was too angry to speak.

"You've got that tick by your eye again," Lila said, reaching up to smooth the frown lines on Gavin's face. "Why didn't you just call me? I'm sure that would have woken me up."

"I did," Gavin said in a low voice. "You left your phone by the stables."

"Oh." She chewed her lip again, her large, hazel eyes nervously glancing between them. God, she was the most beautiful woman he'd ever seen with her wild hair, her large eyes and her little, up-turned nose. "Guess you're both kind of mad about that, huh?"

"You could say that," Gavin drawled.

Trace reached down and picked her up, hauling her against his chest.

"Trace! I can walk."

"Last time you stood up, you fainted. I ain't putting you on your feet, honey. So just hush up and rest. We'll have you back home and in your bed as quick as we can." Besides, he liked holding her in his arms. When he held her, he felt at peace, like he was home. He didn't have the social skills that Colin did, or the sheer force of personality that Gavin had. Trace was a bit of a loner, he preferred the company of horses to most humans, but Lila and his brothers were his world. He didn't want to imagine a life without them in it.

They rode home slowly. Trace held Lila before him on his horse, while Gavin led Sunshine. As the house came into view, they all gave a sigh of relief. Trace pulled his horse to a stop outside the stables. Ron came out quickly, peering up at them in concern as Gavin dismounted and reached for Lila.

"She okay?" he asked.

"I'm fine, Ron," Lila told him warmly as Gavin held her against his chest. "I just wish these two would believe me."

"She fainted," Trace explained as he dismounted. "Gavin, you take her inside and get her settled, I'll take care of the horses." He knew Gavin needed some time alone with Lila to reassure himself that she was fine. The thing about a relationship like they wanted was that no one could be selfish. They always had to think about what was in Lila's best interest first then each other second.

Trace would have his own time with Lila, but right now, Gavin needed to be with her more.

GAVIN CARRIED Lila up the stairs carefully, holding onto her tightly without smothering her against his chest. Terror had nearly stopped his heart when he'd seen her collapse. The idea of losing her... No, it wouldn't happen. He couldn't let her go. He wouldn't.

She'd stay here, letting them protect and cuddle and love her.

"You know you're in trouble for this, don't you?" he told her quietly as he entered her bedroom and placed her on the bed. She immediately tried to sit up, but he pushed her gently back.

"Lie down, you're not going anywhere." He reached down and pulled off her boots, reaching for her pants next.

Lila slapped his hands away. "Gavin! What do you think you're doing?"

"I'm getting you undressed and into bed."

"I don't need to go to bed. I want some food and a swim."

"You're going to bed," he growled. "I'll get you some food once you're lying down quietly. You just fainted dead away, there is no way in hell you're going for a swim right now. So just lie still and let me take care of you."

"But I'm all hot and sticky," she complained.

"I'll get you a washcloth in a moment." He reached for her pants again, tugging them down despite her wiggling and protests. As soon as he had them off, displaying her lacy, purple underwear to his gaze, she scooted back, trying to dive off the opposite side of the bed.

But he was too quick for her and snatching her leg, he pulled her slowly, carefully back towards him.

"Damn it, Gavin," she complained as he dragged her down over the bed. Her bottom was too much temptation to pass up, especially when he saw that those purple panties were actually a

G-string, and Gavin gave her a few hard smacks before rubbing the sting in.

"Behave." He turned her over.

"What was that for?" she asked him, eyes wide with shock.

Gavin reached for her top, pulling it quickly over her head, ignoring her protests. He swallowed, all too aware of the heavy erection pressing against the zipper of his pants. But he couldn't give in to his urge to take her. Not yet. She'd just fainted for God's sake. He should be taking care of her, not imagining himself sinking deep inside her.

He walked over to her drawers, opening a few before he found a long T-shirt. Turning back, he was gratified to find her sitting where he'd left her. Hell, maybe he ought to spank her each morning, at least then she might stay where he put her.

He smiled at the thought.

"What's so funny? You find hitting me funny?"

"I didn't hit you, I gave you a few warning smacks on your butt to calm you down," he told her. She blushed at his words and he watched her carefully, certain she was aroused. Her nipples were pressing against her lacy bra which perfectly matched the G-string. Had those few spanks he'd given her turned her on? Hmm... Who knew their little tomboy liked pretty lingerie? Although the panties and bra she currently wore looked a bit worse for wear. The panties had a hole at the seam.

He made a mental note to do some shopping for her. His baby deserved the best he could buy her.

He helped her sit up. "Arms up."

"Gavin, I'm not five. I can put a t-shirt on," she said with exasperation, her cheeks still red. Gavin just held on to the t-shirt and stood there, waiting. Finally, glaring at him, she did as ordered and he slipped it on.

"Do you need to go to the bathroom?" She shook her head and he frowned, wondering if she was dehydrated.

"Wait there. I catch you out of that bed and you'll be getting a second spanking on top of the one you're already owed."

Her jaw dropped open and she just stared after him as he walked into the attached bathroom and grabbed a face cloth, wetting it under the tap. When he returned to the bedroom he was gratified to find her sitting where he'd left her.

He was going to roast her butt for leaving her phone behind. Even if it had been an accident, she should have double-checked that she had it before she left.

"You have no reason to spank me," she told him indignantly as he sat beside her and washed her face with the cool cloth, moving it down her neck.

"You agreed to our rules, baby girl. And you know you were supposed to take your phone with you. If Ron didn't tell us where you had headed off to, we could still be out there, searching for you. That's unacceptable, Lila."

He blamed himself. He'd seen how exhausted she was this morning at breakfast. He should have been firmer with her and insisted she stay home and rest today. He wiped her hands.

"I'm sorry, but I didn't mean to leave it behind. I just wanted to have some time to myself, to think."

And he could understand that. They'd hit her with a lot at a time when she was emotionally vulnerable. It wasn't fair and their timing was terrible, but circumstances had forced them to move quicker than they would have liked.

"I know this is a lot to take in, baby, and I'm sorry we told you everything on the day of Clay's funeral. We should have held back, but we couldn't let you leave."

She nodded. "I want to stay here and explore what's between the four of us. But it's all so much to take in. Sorry."

He tucked two fingers under her chin and raised her face, kissing her on the lips. "Don't be sorry for how you feel. You can tell me anything. Believe me, baby, I want to make this work and I will do anything to ensure your happiness."

"Really?" she said with a calculated look. "Anything? So you won't be spanking me anymore?"

Gavin chuckled. "Good try, baby girl, but no cigar." He brushed his fingers over her cheek. "Don't you understand how precious you are to us? Trace and I were nearly out of our minds with worry, especially when you didn't answer your phone. When we found it by the stables, I nearly threw up. I imagined every possible bad scenario."

"I'm sorry," she whispered, squeezing his hand. "I'll be more careful next time."

He patted her hand. "You stay there and rest, I'm going to go get us some lunch and something to drink."

Stepping into the kitchen, Gavin took a deep breath and tried to calm himself. Now that he had her back home and safe in her bed, he was starting to crash, his adrenaline rush draining away.

"How is she?" Trace asked coming through the kitchen door.

"Good, more color in her cheeks. She's tucked into bed. I was just going to get us some lunch."

"She scared me. When I think about something happening to her..." Trace trailed off. Gavin turned to him and clapped him on the back, the manly equivalent of a hug.

"She'll be okay," Gavin reassured her. "We'll make sure of it."

"My hands are itching to burn her butt for not taking her phone with her."

Gavin snorted and piled a tray high with sandwiches, water and iced tea. "You and me both, bro, in fact, I already gave her a few warning swats. As soon as she's feeling better that ass is mine."

Trace nodded. "I think I'll give the doctor a call, make an appointment. It was probably just exhaustion but I'd be happier if the doc looked her over."

"Good thinking. I'll take her in tomorrow morning."

"I can stick around this afternoon if you have things to do, keep an eye on her."

Gavin nodded, grateful his brother was here. That was a plus side of sharing a woman, one of them could usually be around to give her extra attention when she needed it.

Whether she thought she did or not.

5

Colin shook off his fatigue as he pulled into his driveway. The first day he'd arrived here, in Clay's truck with Gavin and Trace beside him, Colin had been a fearful, scrawny eleven-year-old. He'd been terrified about where they were going, about the big man who was now his guardian.

When his parents died he'd been understandably devastated, suddenly his whole world was turned upside down as he found himself in a foster home with strangers who didn't really care if he got enough to eat or went to bed on time or did his homework. If it hadn't been for Trace and Gavin he knew things could have gone horribly wrong for him. He'd been scrawny for his age, easy pickings for older kids.

He was grateful they'd kept him and Trace together. If they'd moved them to another home they might have been separated. Clay had come for them before that happened.

He'd saved them.

Colin stopped his truck and looked at the house that had become his home.

"Miss you," he whispered. "More than you will ever know. Thank you for my family."

His family. Trace, Gavin and Lila.

A surge of energy raced through him at the thought of Lila inside. He was nervous that this couldn't last, worried constantly that she'd change her mind, but he couldn't help but be excited about coming home to her. He climbed out of his truck and walked into the house, washing his hands in the mudroom and taking off his boots before stepping into the kitchen.

Gavin was there, cooking something that smelled delicious. Roast beef. Trace and Lila were nowhere to be seen.

"Hey, man, where are Lila and Trace?" he asked.

Gavin turned to look at him, his face tired.

"What's wrong?" Colin asked.

"Nothing," Gavin sighed. "Sorry, just been a long day. Lila's upstairs in bed. Trace is having a shower."

"In bed?" Colin queried.

"Yeah. She fainted today."

"What?" Fear surged through him. "Is she okay? What did the doctor say?"

"Got an appointment first thing in the morning. She's okay, irritated at having to go to bed, but she's slept most of the afternoon so I know she needs it." Gavin told Colin what happened.

Worry churned in his gut. "I'll go up there, keep her company while you're cooking dinner."

He raced up the stairs without waiting for Gavin's reply, slowing at the last moment before bursting through the door, remembering that she may very well be sleeping. He stepped inside to find her out of bed and staring out the window. The T-shirt she wore barely covered her ass and he caught glimpses of her firm, round butt.

"Are you supposed to be out of bed, Lila?" he drawled, crossing his arms over his chest as he leaned back against the door.

She gasped and turned, one hand covering her chest, while the other went to the hem of her T-shirt, trying to tug it down. "Colin! You scared me, have you ever heard of knocking?"

"I figured you'd be asleep."

Wrinkling her nose at him, she moved to the bed, sitting on the side. "I'm sick of lying around. It's boring."

She looked better than she had this morning though, he noticed. Her cheeks held some color and those dark patches beneath her eyes had lightened. Seemed like an afternoon in bed was precisely what the doctor ordered.

"You look better," he agreed. "But you did faint today. It's been a tough few weeks, Lila. You need to give yourself a chance to recover."

"You guys have been through the same stuff I have. I don't notice you lying around in bed all day."

"But we haven't just recovered from a bad viral infection," he reminded her, coming to sit beside her. "Tell you what," he tapped her nose, "you hop back into bed and when I'm finished in the shower I'll come and carry you downstairs for dinner."

She rolled her eyes, but nodded. Colin grabbed her legs, tugging them up into the bed. Leaning down, he kissed her. Intending it to be just a small, sweet kiss, he was surprised when she opened her mouth, her arms wrapping around his neck as she pulled him closer.

Colin worried about whether this is what she really wanted. Or whether she'd change her mind once she experienced the reality of being in a relationship with three men.

He needed to get her into bed with them, show her how much she could enjoy three men. Then she'd never leave.

"I'm so happy you're sticking around, babe," he told her.

She smiled, a little nervous. "Me too."

Colin brushed a finger over her nipple, she shivered as it hardened. Just then her stomach growled. He grinned as she blushed.

"I'm hungry."

"Well, milady, let me go see about your dinner."

"Why, thank you, kind sir," she teased with a smile. Damn, she was beautiful with dark curls resting around her head and those wide, innocent eyes.

"I want to give you whatever you need."

"Oh, well then, what I really need is to convince Gavin that he doesn't need to spank me."

Colin chuckled as he turned to walk out of the room. At the door, he turned around, safely out of her reach. "And miss out on seeing that delicious ass of yours turning bright red? I don't think so. And Lila, you might not believe it, but a spanking is something you definitely need."

He quickly left the room before she could retaliate.

LILA LEFT the doctor's office the next morning, Gavin beside her, his hand resting on the small of her back.

"I could have paid the bill myself, Gavin," she said with exasperation. Although she really did need to get a job.

He snorted, ignoring her protest. "Want to stop at the diner for a coffee?"

"Don't you have to get back?" she asked with surprise. She loved spending time with him, any of them, but didn't want to hold him up.

Last night after dinner she'd cuddled up on the sofa with Colin and Gavin as Trace had cleaned up the kitchen. None of them would even hear of her helping. She'd basked in their attention, thrilled to just be with them.

"I have a bit of time. I thought you might enjoy some time away from the ranch."

She hadn't really been into town since she'd been back, other than to drive through on her way to the hospital to visit Clay.

"That would be nice."

They were soon sitting in a booth, a large slice of pie and two steaming cups of coffee sitting before them. Peggy, the owner, had given her a large hug when she'd walked in. She'd owned this place for years and Lila had always liked the older woman.

She dropped her gaze to the piece of pie, feeling sad.

"What's wrong, baby?" Gavin asked gently.

Lila raised her face. "Just remembering the first time Clay brought me here for pie. I'd never eaten at a diner before, never tasted pie either."

"He was a good man," Gavin agreed. "He didn't have to take in a surly, attitude-filled fifteen-year-old boy, but he accepted me without a word of complaint. We must have pushed his temper so many times. I mean, he had an easy, bachelor life, then one day he comes home to find his best friend dead. And suddenly he has a household full of teenage boys. It's a wonder he didn't kill us."

"Or wallop you every day."

"And twice on Sunday's." Spooning her up some pie, he held it to her mouth.

She looked around. "Ahh, do you think you should be doing that?"

"What? Feeding you?"

A flush covered her cheeks. "Well, won't people think it's strange? I mean, we're practically brother and sister."

He raised a brow. "But we're not, and our feelings towards each other are not what a brother and sister feel. Did you really think we were going to hide how we felt for you, Lila?"

"Ahh, well, I mean, what will people think when they see me with each of you?"

He leaned back, staring at her. "Since when do you care about what people think?"

"Since I don't want you guys to suffer!" she whispered back. "You have businesses to run, Colin and Trace, especially. I don't want to do anything to wreck that."

Gavin cupped her chin with his hand. "Honey, we would never allow that to happen, just like we would never allow anyone to disrespect you. You know there are plenty of ménage relationships here."

"I know." Her friend Laken had two dads. "But this is a little different, isn't it?"

"Because we grew up in the same household? Baby girl, no one is going to even blink at that, I promise. And if anyone ever said anything to you then you would tell one of us straight away, wouldn't you?"

She frowned slightly.

"Lila," he warned. "Listen to me now. We are responsible for you. That means that if anyone is causing you any problems, we expect you to tell us about it."

"I don't want you to handle all my problems, Gavin," she said, even though the thought of having them to lean on was undeniably attractive.

"Do you remember Logan and Max Ferguson?" Gavin asked suddenly.

She frowned slightly, wondering what the Ferguson brothers had to do with anything. "Sure they're friends with Colin."

"Yep. And Colin was best man at their wedding to Savannah last year."

She felt her jaw drop open. "Both of them? They share her?"

He smiled. "Sure do. In fact the number of ménage relationships in Haven is growing. You know we're a bit more open-minded around here. Having a partner means the men have help protecting and caring for their woman, and the women, well, they don't complain." He winked at her.

Lila nodded. Once, her car had broken down as she was

driving herself and Laken home from school. Mac Donaldson, who was a friend of Clay's, had stopped and fixed her car, scolding her for not calling Clay immediately.

She'd called Clay at Mac's insistence and he'd come out to meet them, following them home to make sure they made it there safely. At the time, she and Laken had rolled their eyes, but secretly she'd felt warm at how Clay and Mac had taken care of them, like they'd been important.

"So no one will be that surprised by our relationship. Now, have some pie. The doctor said you're too thin."

She snorted. "That's because he took a litre of blood from me."

"He's just checking to make sure you're well."

"I'm fine," she protested, but took the mouthful of apple pie. "He said I fainted from a combination of too much sun and fatigue."

"I know." Gavin had insisted on coming into the doctor's office with her. "But it doesn't hurt to get you all checked out. He said you refused the tests last time I took you." Gavin scowled. "I knew I should have gone inside with you."

She sighed but had to smile. Gavin was incredibly overprotective. And she loved him just the way he was.

"When was the last time you had a proper check-up?" he asked.

Lila squirmed on her seat. "Before I left for college, Clay took me to get some, umm, pills."

Gavin raised his eyebrow. "Pills for what?"

She wished she could refuse to answer him, but he had that look on his face that told her he wasn't going to allow her to refuse him.

"The Pill. For birth control."

He nearly choked on the sip of coffee he'd just taken. "Say what? Clay took you to get birth control pills?"

A grin curved her lips up. "Yep, I'm not sure which one of us was more embarrassed when he brought it up. Of course, that wasn't as bad as the conversation we had about periods." Now her cheeks were bright red. "Lord, that was bad. And when he had to explain about tampons, I thought we'd both self-combust we were so embarrassed."

Gavin just looked at her and shook his head. "Christ, I never even thought about that stuff. He was an amazing man."

"He sure was."

Gavin looked at his watch and sighed. "I suppose we better head back. I'll just go pay the bill and go to the bathroom."

He squeezed her hand and slipped out of the booth. He laughed with Peggy as he paid. As he moved into the bathroom, she stood and went to speak with Peggy.

"Hey, Peggy, don't suppose you have any jobs going?" she asked.

Peggy screwed up her face. "I'm sorry, sweetie, I've got a full roster. Don't know of anyone hiring, either."

"That's okay," she said, disappointed. Maybe she'd have to try the next town over. Which meant getting a car, which was another hassle and expense in itself.

"I'll be sure to keep an ear out, honey."

Lila smiled. She loved the way this town worked, how they all took care of each other. They didn't suffer fools, but they knew how to look out for their own.

"Thanks," Lila replied.

She turned to find Gavin standing behind her. He grabbed hold of her hand, pulling her along with him as they left the diner. He opened the passenger seat and helped her into his truck.

He started up the truck, pulling it out of the parking lot. "What is Peggy keeping an ear out for?"

"Hmm? Oh, for a job. She doesn't know of any but she'll let me know if anything comes up."

Gavin scowled, glancing over at her. "Why do you need a job?"

"Ahh, because I need money?" She'd have thought that fairly obvious.

"We have plenty of money."

"That's your money. I want my own money."

"Well, I was kind of hoping you'd help with the bookwork at the ranch. You know how much I hate that."

It was true, he detested bookwork. Everyone knew to stay out of Gavin's way when he was doing the accounts.

"I'd be happy to help out with the bookwork, but I don't expect you to pay me for that."

He frowned. "If you're working for me then I'm paying you, baby, and I don't want to hear another word about it."

"And I say you've already done enough. You guys are paying all the bills and groceries, hell; you're even paying my doctor's bills. I don't want you paying me, Gavin."

He growled. "We'll see."

Yes, they would.

TWO NIGHTS LATER, Lila followed Gavin and Trace into the house. They'd just taken her out to Frieda's for dinner, one of only two restaurants in town.

She walked into the living room and threw herself down on the couch after dinner. "I am stuffed."

"Me too," Trace groaned, patting his stomach.

She'd been surprised by how many people had stopped to talk to her tonight. She supposed they'd been at the funeral, but she'd been in a bit of a daze that day. No one had acted shocked by the way Trace and Gavin touched her constantly.

They took every chance they could to touch her, in fact, and even though their caresses remained over her clothing, Lila was about ready to burst with need.

And if the hard erections she often felt pressing against her were any indication, then her men felt the same way. She'd been thoroughly spoilt, although they never missed an opportunity to remind her that she had a punishment coming her way, something that filled her with a mix of dread and curiosity.

The only downside of the night was that Colin had been unable to join them.

Gavin turned to her. "We'll give your dinner a chance to go down and then we'll address the spanking you have coming."

And just like that she forgot about the discomfit of her stomach and started to think about the comfort of her butt.

"Gavin, you really don't need to spank me. I won't forget my phone again, I promise."

He stared at her seriously for a long moment. "And a spanking will help you remember. You know the rules. You put yourself in danger or risk your health and your butt gets spanked."

She chewed her lip, watching him nervously. "I'm scared."

Trace took her hand. "None of us would ever abuse you. I hope you know that."

Lila nodded. "I do. I know it."

"Then trust us," he continued. "Yeah, your butt is going to pay, but if it makes you think twice next time about checking where your phone is then it's worth it."

She took a deep breath. They needed this from her. Hell, a part of her kind of figured she did too.

"Come here, baby." Gavin patted his lap. But instead of pulling her over his lap as she'd expected, he tugged her to sit on his knees and held her tight, rocking her.

"Don't ever be scared of me, please?"

"I won't." She couldn't be. They were hers. All three of them.

Gavin kissed her, taking her mouth, slipping his tongue inside to play with hers until she was breathing harshly.

He then helped her stand. "Okay, baby girl. Strip off your pants and panties then over my lap."

She blushed, embarrassed. "I have to take my panties off?"

"I only give bare-bottomed spankings."

Horribly embarrassed, especially with Trace watching on, and yet feeling more than a little aroused, Lila let Gavin took her hand and help her settle over his lap.

GAVIN LOOKED DOWN at Lila's gorgeous round bottom and his mouth went dry. Damn, she was beautiful. Suddenly, it was hard to hold on to his resolve to give her a sharp reminder to be more careful with her safety.

He ran his hand over her bottom and she grew tense. But he simply rubbed her butt in long, lazy circles until she relaxed.

Clearing his throat, he looked up and saw the wry look Trace sent him. It helped to know his brother was feeling the same way. The last thing he wanted to do right now was spank her.

"I know you're new to this, baby girl, so I'm going to go through the rules. You may yell and cry out but you may not swear or be disrespectful, that will only get you extras. I expect you to do your best to stay in place. You may not hit me or bite me. There is no reaching back with your hands; if you can't hold them before you then Trace will hold them for you."

"No, I can do it."

"All right then." He slapped his hand down with slow, steady movements until her bottom was a pretty pink. Lila lay still over his lap, her only reaction a slight hitch in her breath.

Gavin rubbed her bottom, spreading the heat. "Damn, your ass looks even more beautiful when it's blushing red."

Lila looked back at him questioningly. This was a bad idea. He should continue to spank her, show her how serious he was about her safety. But...

"This was partly my fault," he admitted. "You were exhausted, which is why you fell asleep. If I'd insisted you stay home and rest you wouldn't have fainted."

"Does that mean I get to spank you next?" she asked cheekily.

He shook his head. "No way, brat. But it does mean I'm having trouble really spanking you."

She pouted. "It feels like a real spanking."

Gavin sighed, continuing to pat her softly. He gave her five more sharp, hard slaps. Then rolled her over, sitting her up, careful to make sure that her bottom didn't touch his hard lap.

"You okay, baby girl?" he asked gently.

"Yes, just..."

He noticed the way she shifted around on his lap. Hmm, could it be that spanking turned her on? Interesting.

"Are you wet, Lila?"

She stilled then stared up at him, her eyes wide. "What?"

"You think she's aroused?" Trace asked, his voice husky.

"I think that our girl is turned on from being spanked."

"Am not."

He raised one eyebrow. "Are you saying that if Trace parted those lips, he wouldn't find them gushing with cream?"

"Oh Lord, you can't say things like that." Her cheeks filled with red but there was interest in her gaze.

"Well?" Trace asked. "Are you wet, Lila?"

"No!"

"Tut-tut," Gavin told her. "Lying will get you in more trouble. Now Trace is going to have to check."

They pulled her down so that just her upper body lay on him, her legs resting on the couch.

"No...wait...oh my God." She stiffened in his arms as Trace spread her legs wide, sitting so he pinned one leg against the sofa with his body, holding the other leg down with one hand.

"Oh, that is a beautiful sight," he said.

Gavin's arousal grew, his need for her so great he thought he might explode.

Trace reached down with his free hand and parted her lips. Gavin wished he had the view Trace did. He just knew her lips would be plump, pink, perfect. Trace ran one finger up and down her slit and she jumped then groaned.

He held his finger up, it glistened under the lights. "Definitely aroused."

"What a naughty girl to lie about your arousal," Gavin told her, flicking one tight nipple.

She gasped.

"You wouldn't get to come because this was a punishment spanking, but now, Trace is going to have to give you a few more spanks for lying."

"What? No!"

Trace released her legs, pushing them up to her chest. Gavin placed his arm behind her knees, holding them pressed against her.

"Fuck, that's a beautiful sight." Trace smacked his hand against her ass and she cried out.

"Please, no more. I can't stand it. I have to come."

"No coming," Gavin told her.

Trace finished and rubbed her ass. "Beautiful."

Gavin sighed. What he wouldn't give to sink his hard cock deep inside her. He just knew she would feel like heaven around him. But she wasn't ready yet.

He stood, holding her in his arms as he carried her up the stairs. Trace stood, placing a kiss on her lips as they walked past. Gavin hadn't thought it possible to love her any more, but he felt his chest swelling.

He set her on the side of the bed and moved to her drawers to grab one of his T-shirts that she'd taken to wearing to bed. She'd stolen a shirt from each of them out of the laundry. Not that any of them were complaining. He loved the thought of her wearing his T-shirt to bed. Of course, he loved the thought of her naked, in his bed, more. Walking back over, he handed it to her.

"You get ready for bed, baby girl. I'll be back in soon."

"Wait. Don't you want to join me?" she asked.

He turned back. "More than anything. But it isn't time yet."

"It isn't? It sure feels like it."

He grinned and then leaned down to kiss her. "Soon. I promise. Before we all explode."

He walked out quickly. He wanted nothing more than to take her into his arms and kiss her, to worship those breasts and spread her legs so he could lick the lush cream from her folds.

But he had to wait. She wasn't ready. Not yet.

Damn it was hard.

He paced up and down the passage before knocking and entering her room. She was lying in bed.

Gavin walked over to her bookshelf and pulling down an old favorite, sat in the armchair by her bed.

"Are you going to read to me?" she asked.

It was something Clay had always done when she was feeling upset or lonely.

"I sure am, precious. You just lie back, close your eyes and listen."

Gavin started reading. She was asleep by page five, but he stayed there, just watching her sleep for a long time.

Lila woke up slowly, she stretched, surprised to find that her bottom no longer hurt. She'd still expected to feel the effects of last night's spanking. Reaching down, she massaged her bottom. Her eyes shot open as a low chuckle filled the room. She glanced over to find Trace sitting in the chair that Gavin had been sitting in last night.

"Sore, little girl?" he asked in a low voice.

She scowled at him. "Not really, although I thought I would be. You both have hands like wooden blocks."

Trace grinned and leaning forward, pushed her hair back off her face. "Pff, we went easy on you."

Easy? Hell's bells.

She coughed a little, her mouth dry. Trace reached over and grabbed a glass of water, holding it as she sat up. She took it gratefully. "Thanks."

She put the empty glass down on the table, frowning slightly.

"Something wrong?"

"I just...I'm worried about looking after the three of you. Three men to look after is a lot when I'm not used to even one man. I mean, what if Colin and Gavin get jealous of you being in here with me, I mean, I don't think I can handle keeping track..." she started to grow panicky.

"Shh, honey," Trace soothed her. "You aren't to worry about any of that stuff, okay? We won't get jealous and if that ever did happen then it would be between us. We all want time alone with you, of course, but we'll work that out. I know it seems pretty intimidating, especially since we're all fairly hard-headed men, but just remember that you know us.

"We are always here for you. The good thing about having three men is that one of us will always be available to you. If you need a hug or some advice or that jar of pickles opened, then one of us will be there. You just have to ask. We are here for you, Lila girl."

"I'll do my best never to hurt you guys, too." She looked down at her hands. "Is Colin home yet?"

"Yes, baby, he came home last night. Hey, why so sad?" Trace placed his fingers under her chin, raising her face.

"Did he really have to work last night?"

Trace looked surprised then he sighed. "Yes, he did."

"Why do I feel like he doesn't really want to be seen with me? Is he ashamed of me?" She hated how insecure she felt, but she had to know.

Trace gathered her into his arms. "No, God, no. Never think that." He kissed the top of her head then set her back. "This is something you need to talk to Colin about."

"I feel sick at the idea that he doesn't want to be around me."

Trace kissed her. "He loves you, I know he does. But about eight months ago he was hurt badly. Hocken lost one of their vets, so Colin was helping them out two days a week. He was really enjoying it, even though it was a bit of a drive going to Hocken and back."

"He had this assistant, Sara. She had the hots for him, it was easy to see when we met her, but he wouldn't listen to me or Gavin. He just figured she was being friendly. You know what Colin's like, he's friends with everyone."

She nodded. Colin did tend to try and see the good in everyone. Or he had, she sensed something had changed about him. He'd become harder.

"Well, she started to get pushier and bitchier when he didn't buy what she was trying to sell. He returned to his motel room one night to find her in his bed. She threw herself at him. Colin tried to let her down gently, so he explained about our feelings for you."

She winced. "Oh, crap."

Trace smiled wryly. "Exactly. She went off, called him a pervert, an asshole and worse. But she didn't stop there. She started spreading lies, telling everyone that he'd tried to force her into a relationship with all of us. She had a lot of friends and the community didn't react well. In the end he couldn't even walk down the street without someone commenting. Gavin and I could have handled it, but not Colin. He was devastated. Even though he knows no one in Haven would say anything or even think anything bad, the fear is still there."

"Poor Colin," she whispered. "That's horrible."

"Yes, but he has no right to make you feel unwanted. I'll have a chat with him." His face grew grim and she grabbed his hand.

"No, don't, please. Just let it be. Promise me."

Looking reluctant, he nodded. "Okay, I'll leave it. So long as he doesn't hurt you."

"How is she?" Gavin asked Trace as he walked into the kitchen.

"She's good. Still a bit worried about how the relationship between the four of us would work, but I think I eased her mind."

"What relationship?" Colin said with frustration. "We haven't done more than kiss her. She'll probably change her mind. I mean, what woman would really want the three of us? I should have known this idea was crazy, that it would never work. But I let you guys talk me around. It's never going to work."

"It will work, if we all stick together. Don't let what happened with Sara affect your relationship with Lila," Gavin urged. He held back his temper. He knew Colin had been hurt badly by what had happened in Hocken, but he wasn't about to let Colin ruin this for them or hurt Lila.

"She wants us," Trace reassured him in a far more patient voice than Gavin could manage. "She loves us, Colin. She just wants to take it slow, is that so hard to understand?"

"No sane woman would want what we want, they'd think it disgusting."

Gavin placed his hands on his hips, but before he could open his mouth Trace caught his eyes, shaking his head. Trace turned to his younger brother.

"I can tell you right now that Lila certainly didn't look

disgusted last night when she danced between me and Gavin at Dirty Delights last night," Trace told him.

"You went dancing at Dirty Delights?" Colin asked.

Gavin relaxed slightly at the disappointment on Colin's face. He did want this. He was just too scared to believe in it yet. "If you'd come with us, you'd know she's not ashamed or horrified by what we want and neither is anyone else. Were you disgusted by Max, Logan and Savannah?"

"That's different," Colin insisted. "I know the people here won't turn their back on me, but will Lila be able to live like this or is the novelty going to wear off?"

"I'm not her, Colin. I will try my hardest not to hurt you."

They all turned at Lila's voice.

Fuck, how long had she been standing there? She wore an old pink robe, her hair mussed around her face, her eyes still a bit heavy with sleep. And she looked so adorable that Gavin wanted to grab her and spirit her off to bed.

Gavin opened up his arms. "Come here, baby girl," he told her, gratified when she didn't hesitate to fling herself into his arms. He glared at Colin.

Trace came up behind her. He ran his hand down her back, obviously feeling the shudders racking her slight body as he looked up at Gavin in concern. "Why aren't you in the shower?"

"I wanted to talk to you guys and I didn't want to lose my nerve. I don't want to cause any arguments between all of you. I don't want to hurt anyone. Maybe it would be best if I just left."

Gavin squeezed her tight, terror filling him at the thought of losing her. "Like hell." He looked at his brothers. They stared back at him, faces filled with worry. Placing his hands under her butt, he hoisted her into the air. Her legs came around his waist. "Let's get one thing straight right now, precious. You are the most important person in this room. Sometimes we fight amongst ourselves, we're brothers, that's what siblings do. But it is not your fault, you are never to blame. Do you hear me?"

"Lila, whatever we do, you decide the pace of it," Trace told her. "You decide how far we go and when."

She nodded then looked over at Colin who still held himself back. "Let me down, please."

Gavin let her go reluctantly, watching carefully as she walked over to stand in front of Colin.

"I want this," Lila told him. "Being with the three of you is something I take very seriously, which is part of the reason I want to go slow. I'm not holding back from having sex because I'm scared or horrified about being with the three of you, but because I want to build our relationship first. Because once I sleep with you I'm guessing I won't leave your bed for quite a while." Although last night she certainly wouldn't have turned Gavin and Trace away.

Colin remained quiet. "Colin? What are you thinking? Please talk to me."

He shook his head and turning, took off out the door. Lila looked after him, her face devastated.

"Oh God, he doesn't want this, does he?" she asked, looking back at Gavin and Trace, tears in her eyes.

"Give him time, Lila." Trace wrapped his arms around her. "He needs to think things through." They heard a door slamming then the roar of a truck. She winced.

"I don't want to force him."

"None of us do, baby girl." Gavin walked over and clasped her face between his hands. "Colin needs to work things through for himself. Tell you what, how would you like to spend the whole day with us?"

"You have the day off?" she asked in an excited voice, making him smile.

"Yes, baby girl. So how about you go get ready while I get some breakfast together. Then we'll all go for a ride. Would you like that?"

She nodded eagerly then kissed Gavin's lips before raising her face up for Trace to kiss her. "That sounds great."

Gavin smiled as she left. He only hoped that Colin could let go of his past enough to let himself enjoy their beautiful girl.

6

_____

Colin drove without really noticing where he was going. He was ashamed of the way he'd just stormed out without even talking to Lila, especially when he pictured her face, filled with sadness and a touch of fear.

As though afraid he would never accept her.

He just found it hard to trust that this is what she really wanted. Part of him expected her to call him a sick bastard, to look at him in disgust. He never wanted to see Lila looking at him the way Sara had. Shaking off old memories, he pulled up outside the Fergusons.

As he climbed out of the truck, Max walked out onto the porch.

"Morning," Max called out. "Bit early to offer you a beer but I have some coffee."

"Thanks man," Colin called out.

Max nodded. "I'll bring it out."

Ten minutes later they were sitting on the wide porch, looking out at the land, cups of cooling coffee held in their hands.

"So how are things?" Max asked casually. "How are your

brothers and Lila?" Colin had confided in Max and Logan years ago about what he and his brothers felt towards Lila. Before Sara had made him feel ashamed of his own feelings.

"Okay," Colin replied, smiling without humor. "Well, except for the fact that I just stormed out in a fit of temper."

Max didn't react, just sat back in his seat. "Not like you to lose your temper."

Colin sighed and, leaning forward, rested his elbows on his knees. "You remember Sara?"

Max snorted. "Yeah, I remember Sara. That woman was a bitch. Savannah hated her."

Colin raised his eyebrows. "She did?" As far as he knew Savannah got on with pretty much anyone. She'd never let on that she disliked Sara when Colin had arranged for them all to meet up. He'd thought he and Sara were good friends. Turned out she'd wanted more, and he'd been naïve. Why did he confide in her about how he and his brothers felt about Lila?

Because he'd trusted her, that's why. And he'd been wrong to. Was he wrong to trust Lila as well?

"Oh yeah, I had to bribe her to spend any time with that woman. I know you thought you guys were friends, but you are better off without friends like that."

Colin blew out a breath. "Yeah, I know. Turns out I wanted a friend and she wanted to get married and have me take care of her."

"So you going to tell me what happened? Don't tell me Sara has popped back up, she's not making trouble with Lila, is she?" Max looked furious at the thought. Colin knew his friend viewed Lila like a little sister—she'd grown up around Max and Logan.

"No, no, the only one causing trouble between me and Lila is me. I'm just having problems believing she really does want to be with all of us."

Max sat back and raised his eyebrows. "Lila is nothing like

Sara. For a start, she's lived in Haven since she was seven. Hell, Laken is her best friend; she spent a lot of nights over there with Laken and her dads. She knows the way Haven works."

Colin nodded, feeling his stomach unravel. He knew all this, but hearing someone else point it all out helped.

"And Lila doesn't play around with people. If it made her uncomfortable, she'd say."

"She told us that she loves us," Colin told him. "It's everything I'd hoped for. But she wants to take things slow. It made me wonder about whether she really wanted this."

"You're a lucky bastard," Max told him. "Hell, you can't blame her for wanting to go slow. She's known you guys for a long time but this is a total shift in your relationship. The fact that you have a history is probably more reason for her to want to take it slow, because if this relationship fails, she doesn't just lose her boyfriends, she loses her home. I'm sure Lila just wants to be sure that you build a good, strong relationship."

Sighing, Colin ran his hand over his face tiredly. "You're right. And I took her need to go slow as a rejection. God, I'm an asshole. I just can't seem to get Sara's words out of my head. I really hurt Lila today."

"Lila's a tough nut. She's been through a lot and I'm sure she has her own triggers. I think she'll understand. One thing I've learned since meeting Savannah is that if a woman loves you then she'll forgive a lot, but only if you talk to her."

Colin sighed, nodding his head. "You're right. I know you're right. I need to talk to her. I have to work past this before it mucks everything up."

"Sounds to me like you're this close to having it all." Max held his finger and thumb an inch apart. "You just have to make that jump. It's a leap of faith. You need to trust her to catch you, just like you'd catch her."

"Damn, when did you get to be such a smart bastard?" Colin said with a grin. Max punched him on the shoulder, laughing.

A phone rang and Max stood, going inside to answer it. Colin took another sip of his coffee and realized how stupidly he'd behaved. Now he just had to figure out how to make it up to Lila.

Max returned to the front porch, a small frown on his face.

"Something wrong?" Colin asked.

"That was Jake. He just pulled Savannah up doing fifty in a thirty-five zone," he said with a scowl.

Colin let out a low, long whistle. "Somebody's bottom is going to be toast."

Max grinned. "So are you going to go home and make up with Lila?"

"Yep, I'll even get down on my knees if I have to."

"I'm glad. You all deserve to be happy. I know things haven't been easy lately, but Clay would be pleased."

"I know. He loved all of us. All he wanted was for us to be happy."

"He was a great man. Have you had the reading of the will yet?"

Colin shook his head. "No, we've got an appointment with the lawyer next Tuesday."

A small blue car moved slowly up the driveway. Colin cracked a smile. "Seems like someone has learned to slow down."

Max snorted. "Oh, she'll learn all right." But he stood with a smile and went down to greet his wife, opening her door and giving her a kiss, before grabbing her shopping and carrying the bags inside.

Short and curvy with blonde hair, Savannah had a ready smile and a cheerful disposition. No one could remain grouchy for long with her around.

"Colin," she squealed, throwing her arms around him. "How are you? How are your brothers?"

"We're all good Savi, how are you, sweetheart?"

"I'm good," she replied. "All of you should come over for dinner one night. I only met Lila briefly at the funeral and I doubt she remembers me."

"We'd like that," he replied warmly.

Max returned from putting the packages inside and held out his arms. "Come here, love," he crooned to her.

She immediately bounced over to him, throwing herself into his arms. He kissed the top of her head, his heart filling his eyes. "Have a good time in town?"

"Oh well, as much excitement as you can have grocery shopping," she said.

Colin grinned, knowing she couldn't see him. Savi was a terrible liar and it wouldn't take Max long to ferret the truth out of her.

"Yeah? Talk to anyone while you were there?" Max asked.

"Well, just old Joe and Sally," she said slowly. Then with a sigh she pulled back and looked up at Max, her face resigned. "Jake called you, didn't he?"

"Yes, love, he did."

"I'm sorry," she said quickly. "I didn't mean to, I didn't even notice my speed creeping up."

Max ran his hand over her hair. "I know, but this isn't the first time, is it? You put your safety at risk and that's unacceptable."

She wrinkled her nose.

Max whispered something in her ear and she blushed bright red, shifting her weight from leg to leg before glancing over at Colin. He had to work hard to hide his smile.

With a blush covering her cheeks, she sped inside.

As soon as she was gone, Colin let out a chuckle. "You could fry eggs on those cheeks of hers."

Max nodded. "And soon I'll be able to fry eggs on her other

cheeks. This has to stop. She's been getting away with murder lately, simply because we've been so busy."

"Maybe you should start spanking her each morning as a preventative measure," Colin joked.

Max looked thoughtful. "The idea has merit."

A dark blue truck pulled up beside Colin's truck, and Max's twin brother, Logan climbed out.

"Colin, good to see you man." Logan held out his hand and Colin shook it. Although the men were twins they looked nothing alike. Where Logan had light brown hair and hazel eyes, Max's hair was almost black, his eyes a dark gray. But they were both large, built wide across the shoulders and standing around six feet three.

"Just came home to get changed," he explained, moving inside. Max and Colin talked for a while until Logan came out ten minutes later.

"What did she do this time?" he asked his brother.

"Caught speeding by Jake. Doing fifty in a thirty-five zone."

Logan scowled. "That's the second time this month."

Max nodded. "I'll take care of it then I'll join you."

"All right. See you later, Colin," Logan called with a wave of his hand.

"Later man." Colin held his hand out to Max. "Thanks for listening and the advice. I better go take care of my girl and leave you to take care of yours."

Max smiled. "Oh, I'm sure she's not eager for me to hurry inside."

Colin laughed. "No, I expect not."

7

L ila thoroughly enjoyed spending the day with Gavin and Trace. It wasn't often that they all had a day off together and she relished the time and attention they lavished on her.

The only dark cloud hanging over the day was that Colin wasn't with them. She wondered how she could get through to him—show him that she wasn't like Sara, that she really wanted this. Well, she guessed she could only do it by being herself. Words probably wouldn't convince him, and even if they could, she didn't know exactly what to say.

So she'd have to show him.

"Colin's home," she called out excitedly as she spotted his truck. She nudged Sunshine into a faster trot and raced towards the stables. "Last one home is a rotten egg!"

"Lila, slow down," Gavin roared, but she ignored him, jumping a small hedge instead of moving through the gap as she normally would have.

Colin walked into the yard and she steered Sunshine towards

him. Pulling her horse up next to him, she held herself back from throwing herself into his arms.

But then he held his arms out and she threw herself off into his arms. She cuddled him tight, arms around his neck, her legs firmly clinging to his waist.

"Colin, I'm so glad you're home."

"Ahh, baby, you feel so good in my arms, I'm so sorry I stormed off like that," he murmured. "So sorry I hurt you."

"I'm just glad you've come back. We can work things through as long as you stay and talk to me."

"I will, no more running off," Colin vowed. "I know that you're nothing like Sara, and I'm sorry for reacting the way I did. It was unfair to you."

"It's okay, I understand." She held him tight.

"Hmm, from the way Gavin and Trace are glaring at you I'm thinking you've got some explaining to do."

She looked over her shoulder to find both men dismounting, looks of displeasure on their faces.

"Uh oh," she muttered.

"Oh, I think that's an understatement," he agreed.

Gavin stood there, hands on his hips. "Lila, what were you thinking? You know better than to race around the house. What if someone had walked out in front of you? And jumping that hedge?" He took a deep breath, trying to calm himself.

"Unacceptable," Trace told her before grabbing her horse and leading it and his own into the stables.

Gavin scowled. "You could have hurt yourself. What if Sunshine hadn't taken that jump?"

"It was hardly much of a jump. I've jumped much higher than that before," she told him before swallowing heavily. Gavin's face went white then red. Then with a pointed look at Colin, he turned away, muttering to himself.

Lila sighed. Damn they could be a bunch of worriers. "I was just excited to see you."

"I appreciate that. But riding that way, especially around the house is dangerous." With a smile he set her down and turned her towards the house. He gave her a couple of quick, sharp pops on the seat of her pants.

"Ow, Colin!" she protested loudly.

"That's for putting yourself at risk. Safety first, Lila. Go on inside now and I'll be in soon." With a final smack that had her scowling and rubbing her buttocks, he sent her off.

WITH A LOUD SIGH OF DISPLEASURE, which had Colin smiling, she stomped off. Colin shook his head. Damn, she was something else. They were going to have their hands full, that's for sure. With a low whistle, he headed off to the stables to help his brothers.

"Everything all right?" Gavin asked as he entered and started taking care of Sunshine.

"Yeah," Colin said. "I was just thinking that I'm glad there are three of us to look after her, she can be a handful."

"Actually, I meant is everything all right with you?" Gavin asked. "Lila is happier than I have seen her in a long time. She's more settled, more open, but you upset her today."

"I know and I'm sorry for acting like an asshole and storming out. It won't happen again."

Gavin fixed him with a hard stared. "See that it doesn't."

LILA HEARD the phone ringing as she poured herself a glass of juice. She ran over, snapping it up.

"Hello," she said breathlessly.

"Yeah, put me on with Clay."

Lila frowned. The voice wasn't one she recognized. Obviously not someone who lived around Haven if they didn't know Clay had died. Pain stabbed her stomach.

"I'm sorry, Clay has passed away. Can I help you?"

"Fuck!" the other woman swore. Lila held the phone away from her ear as expletives continued to fly.

"Who is this?" Lila asked sharply. She wouldn't normally be so rude, but she couldn't imagine Clay being friends with someone who spoke like this.

"I'm an old friend of Clay's. Who's this?"

"I'm his daughter. I'm sorry to give you the news this way." Lila was determined to be polite. A door squeaked open and she looked over her shoulder to see her three men enter.

"His daughter? So did you inherit that big spread of his?"

"I'm sorry?" Lila said stiffly. Immediately, Gavin, Trace and Colin walked towards her, looks of concern on their face.

"Who is it?" Gavin asked.

Lila shook her head, shrugging.

"He owed me some money. I'll be coming to collect."

A dial tone greeted her. "How rude!"

"Who was that?" Trace asked. All three men were staring at her, arms over their chests, looking so alike it made her smile, despite the uneasy feeling in her stomach from that phone call.

"I don't know, but she was really rude. She asked for Clay, said he owed her money and that she would be coming to collect."

Gavin scowled. "Why would Clay owe anyone any money?"

"No idea," she replied.

"Well, if it arrives, you let us take care of it, hear me, Lila?" Gavin ordered.

She nodded. She had no interest in talking to that woman again.

"Come here, baby," Colin cajoled, sitting at the table.

She moved towards him.

"Come sit on my knee." Colin patted his lap. Gavin put together some food while Trace got them all a drink. Then the three men sat at the table. Lunch was laid out, salad, buns and cold chicken.

Colin fed her small bites of food. She felt cherished and taken care of. She didn't know where he'd gone when he'd stormed out earlier, but she was glad he'd come back a lot happier.

"Lila? Lila, are you listening?" Gavin asked.

"Yes, sure." Nope. Not really.

Trace chuckled and got up, placing his plate in the dishwasher before giving her a kiss on the head. "I've got stuff to do. I'll see you later."

She smiled up at him. Gavin did the same and then quickly left, leaving her alone with Colin.

"Colin?"

"Yes?"

"Are we really okay, now?"

He ran his hand over her hair and her eyes closed with the soothing movement. "I'm sorry for storming out earlier. I was too scared to believe that this is what you really want. I thought Sara was my friend, I trusted her and she hurt me badly. So I started to question if my choice to share a woman with my brothers was right or wrong. I went and spoke to Max; he made me see that I was giving her exactly what she wanted. She wanted to hurt me. This is right. You, me, Gavin and Trace and I won't let anyone tell me different. I trust you to tell us if we ever do anything you're not comfortable with. I know you won't play games. I'm so sorry I hurt you, though. Forgive me?"

She smiled. "Of course. I love you."

"Love you, too, shorty."

LILA HELD on to Gavin's hand tightly, Colin on her other side as Trace led the way into the lawyer's office. It had been two weeks since Clay's funeral and she felt calmer, more at peace with herself and their relationship.

"Welcome everyone," old Mr. Marsh greeted them. He'd seemed old when she was a kid, he surely had to be over eighty now. "I'm sorry you're here on such a sad occasion. Clay was a marvelous man."

"That he was," Gavin agreed. Reaching over, she grabbed Trace and Colin's hands, holding on tight.

"Well, I'll get on with it as I'm sure you all have things to do. I'll warn you first, though, that the will is a bit unusual. If it was anyone but Clay I would have strongly advised against what he has done, but he was adamant that this was the best way to go about it. I also have a letter here from him that you all need to read together. First, I'll read the will to you."

Lila tuned out the legal stuff. She wasn't even sure why she had to be here. Clay had to have left the ranch to the boys. Maybe he'd left her something little, though.

"Okay on to the bequests. To Gavin, my rock, the son who made me proud with his steadfastness, his honor, and his courage I leave my land. I know you will protect it and take care of it. To Trace, my calm, unflappable son with a heart of gold, I leave all the horses and stables. You have a rare gift with them."

Okay, so she was starting to understand why the lawyer had said this was an odd will. Sounded like Clay, rather than bequeathing the whole ranch to all three men had sectioned it off.

"To Colin, who could always make me laugh, even as a little kid, I leave all the cattle, dogs and other animals."

Colin smiled.

Mr. Marsh looked at her. "Finally, to Lila, my daughter and the heart of my home, I leave the house, I hope it brings her the stability and security she's always needed."

The four of them looked at each other, dumbfounded.

"But-but, he can't leave me the house," she protested. "The guys should get that."

All the men, including the lawyer, scowled at her.

"These were Clay's last wishes, young lady," old Mr. Marsh scolded. "I hope you're not saying you know better."

"No, sir," she replied, suitably chastised.

"Now, as for the rest of his estate, including his stocks and bonds, he's splitting that four ways between you all. Once that's all settled it should total around the two-million-dollar mark. Now, I'm sure you're all quite surprised by this. It's very unusual and could create problems if one of you wanted to sell your part."

"We won't," Gavin told him firmly.

"That's what Clay said. I'll give you some time to process this and read his letter. First, though, I have some paperwork here for you to sign."

Numbly, Lila worked her way through the paperwork that lawyers seemed to thrive on.

Not only had he left her the house, but also half a million dollars? It was unfathomable. Looking around, she found the boys looked as shocked as she did.

"Now, I'll leave you alone for a bit." He handed a piece of paper to Gavin then left.

"It's not right," she blurted out again. "That's your house more than mine."

"And how do you figure that, Lila?" Trace asked calmly. "Because I think it's everyone's house and Clay left it to the person he wanted to have it."

"Let's see what the letter says," Colin suggested.

Gavin opened it then cleared his voice. "Okay, here goes."

To my three sons and daughter

I couldn't have loved the four of you more if you'd been of my own blood. My only regret in this life is that maybe I didn't tell you enough how proud I was of you all, how much I cherished and loved you. I was never an overly demonstrative man, and talking about my feelings didn't come easy, but I hope you all know how cherished you were.

Gavin, you were a rock from the moment I met you. When Trace came up to me and told me how you'd looked after him and Colin, protected them, cared for them, I knew I couldn't walk away from you. I know I'm leaving my family in safe hands with you protecting them. Loyalty is an admirable quality, son, and you have it in abundance. I firmly believe that you were placed with Trace and Colin because you were meant to be part of this family.

Trace, so calm and mature for your age, you were often the voice of reason in our crazy household. You remind me so much of your father, he was just like you, soft-spoken, sensible with a generosity of spirit. He would have been so proud of the man you have become today. You've always been the first one to put up your hand to help someone else and that made me so proud and I know your parents would be too.

And Colin, my jokester. Now you remind me of your mother. She always had a ready laugh, a kind smile and a joke. She could have me and your father in stitches within minutes. You kept the rest of us from being a bit too serious at times and reminded us that life was for living and for having fun. Never change, my boy. And that's an order.

Lastly, but never least is Lila. Lila, sweetheart, I loved you from the first moment I saw you, all curled up in a ball trying to keep out of the rain. I know you'll be surprised that I left you the house, but I had my reasons. I don't think you ever understood your value. Lila, you were always the heart of our household. You were my daughter in every sense of the word and I hope you understand how precious you are. Sweet, shy and yet fiercely independent, a princess who tried to be a tomboy in order to keep up with the boys. But you never had to. You only ever had to be yourself.

Be yourself and everyone will love you. I promise.

So, by now you're wondering why I split up the property the way I did. It's because the four of you belong together, you always did. I know

I made you boys give Lila a few years to herself, but I figure it's been time enough. You need to claim her. You need to make each other happy and learn to live as a family. Each of you owns an interconnecting part of the property just as you owned a piece of my heart.

Clay.

Lila went into shock. She could feel everything around her slowing as she just concentrated on taking one breath then another.

"Wow, he didn't miss a beat, did he?" Colin said in a surprised voice.

"Sure didn't. He knew us better than we did ourselves," Gavin agreed.

"Lila?" Trace questioned. "Are you all right?"

"I don't feel so good. Can I go home?" she asked quietly.

"Course we can," Gavin told her. "Come on, let's go."

As soon as she got home, Lila raced up to her room. She didn't want to be around anyone at the moment. She needed to think. She threw herself onto her bed, arms over her head, fully expecting a knock on her door to come immediately.

So she was surprised when it didn't come for another twenty minutes.

"Lila, honey?" Trace called out.

"Yes?" she asked.

"Colin's out on a job and Gavin has gone to check on the men. I'm just down in the stables if you need me, okay?"

"Okay, thanks," she said with a mixture of relief and disappointment. She needed some time alone to think and yet, she felt lonely without them here.

"If you need to talk, Lila, I'm here for you."

"I know. I just need some time to myself." She tried to keep her voice steady, but knew there was a tremor that betrayed her.

"Okay, sweetheart. Love you."

"Love you, too."

When the house went silent she rose and wandered downstairs, looking around the house through new eyes. She couldn't believe Clay had left this place to her. When she'd first arrived it had seemed so huge and intimidating. But now it was her home.

Their home.

Because it wasn't just hers, no matter what was on the title. It was theirs.

Tears welled in her eyes as she moved into Clay's office. She hadn't been in here since Clay's death. As far as she knew the only one who came in here now was Gavin, and then only to get something he needed for running the ranch.

It still smelled like Clay. Every year she'd bought him the same cologne. She'd never really known if he liked it or not, but he'd always worn it.

"Oh, Clay, why didn't I tell you how much I appreciated you every day?" she whispered, lying down on the couch. When she'd first arrived, she'd lain on this couch at night, waiting for Clay to finish up his paperwork. Afterwards, he'd pick her up and carry her upstairs, tucking her into bed.

The big, gruff rancher had never once lost his temper with her, or told her to leave him alone.

"Thank you for giving me my family."

GAVIN WALKED into the house to find Trace and Colin sitting in the living room having a beer.

"Hey, where's Lila?" Gavin had been worried about leaving her alone earlier, but Trace had been close by and they'd all figured she needed some space. In fact, they'd kind of felt the same way. The letter from Clay had reawakened the loss and to say they'd been surprised by the way he split the ranch up would be an understatement.

Trace glanced up from the game they were watching on TV. "She's in Clay's study. Thought she needed some time alone. But it's probably been long enough."

With a nod, Gavin headed into Clay's study. For the first time since his foster father's death, he wasn't stabbed in the chest with pain upon entering the room. Reaching the couch, he smiled as he found Lila sprawled on the large, leather couch, looking so tiny against the very masculine furniture.

"Hey, baby."

She turned to look at him with a smile before sitting up. He sat next to her, pulling her close. "I love it in here. I feel like he's here with me."

"I know." He looked around. "Me too."

"Why'd he do it, Gavin? Why'd he split things up that way?"

"Because he wanted to show us that he loved all of us and that we were meant to be together."

She nodded, nibbling at her full lower lip. "I wish I had told him more often how much he meant to me."

"He knew it."

Lila looked down at her lap. "I always held part of myself back. I was always a bit scared of being rejected, but he really did see me as his daughter, didn't he?"

"Yes, baby girl."

A smile crossed her face and she relaxed against him. "So I guess I own this house now. You better not upset me, huh, or you guys could find yourselves out on the street."

Gavin grinned. "That so, brat? And what would constitute upsetting you?"

"Well, definitely spankings."

He placed a hand over her mouth, laughing. "Baby girl, you could own the whole of Texas and I would still roast your ass if I thought you needed it."

Tugging his hand away from her face, she pushed her bottom lip out. "Well, that hardly seems fair. My house, my rules."

"I think it's more, our house, our rules, don't you?"

With a sigh, she gave him a kiss. "Yeah, I like the sound of that."

8

A clap of thunder had her sitting up in fright, her heart pounding in her chest. Rain beat heavily against the roof of the house. Glancing out the window, lightning lit up the sky and she whimpered. Moving blindly, fear guiding her movements, she grabbed Tubby and ran for the bedroom door. Racing down the corridor, she found herself in front of Clay's bedroom door before she even realized what she was doing.

Another boom of thunder sounded, making her cry out. Trembling, she turned and raced into the closest bedroom. Pausing, she shook the fear free. What the hell was she doing? Just as she stepped out of the room there was a long, low rumble of thunder and she spun, racing to the bed.

"What? Who?" Trace mumbled sleepily. She threw herself against him. "Lila, honey? What's wrong? What's the matter? What's happened?"

Thunder struck, rain slashed against the window and she huddled against him, trying to bury herself under him.

"Oh, honey, that's one hell of a storm, isn't it? Hush now.

Damn, you're shaking like a leaf. It's okay, little bit. They're just God's farts remember?"

Yeah, if she hadn't believed that when she was seven then she totally wasn't buying it now. Rain pelted down, fast and heavy as Trace rocked her, running his hand up and down her back. Lila found herself relaxing slightly. Thunder boomed again, making her shudder, but she stayed where she was, safely ensconced in Trace's arms.

"Lila!" She heard Gavin yell. "Where are you?"

"She's in here!" Trace hollered back, causing her to giggle. Leaning over, he flicked the switch on the bedside lamp. Soft light filled the room, helping her fight her fear.

"What's so funny, little bit?" Trace teased, tickling her.

"You guys. Just as well we don't have neighbors; they'd be able to hear all of you over the thunder."

Colin and Gavin barreled through the door then, dressed only in boxer shorts. Muscles and tanned skin filled her vision, almost making her forget about the storm raging outside.

Almost.

Another clap of thunder had her burying her face against Trace. Gavin and Colin climbed in on either side of them as Trace pulled her to lie on top of him.

"You okay, baby girl?" Gavin asked with concern. She buried her face against Trace's chest as she nodded. She remembered so many storms that she'd spent alone, huddled in the closet of her apartment with Tubby, wishing she wasn't alone.

"Lila?" Colin questioned. "Honey, talk to us. Would you rather we went to Clay's room?"

"No, no, I'm okay," she said hastily. "Here is good. Unless I'm too heavy?" She looked up at Trace in concern.

He snorted and gently pushed her head back against his chest. "Don't be silly. Now, relax. The storm is dying off, we're here, and we're not going to let anything happen to you. I promise. Just relax, Lila. Relax."

With the heat of their bodies infusing hers, Lila found her eyes drifting shut. She yawned and snuggled down, letting sleep pull her in.

GAVIN RAN his hand over Lila's back, unable to stop touching her. As soon as he'd been woken by the storm, he'd gone looking for her, knowing she'd need him.

"At least she came here and didn't go straight for a closet," Colin commented from the other side of Trace.

"It's where I looked first," Gavin admitted.

Lila had only been living with them for about a month when they'd had their first thunderstorm. She'd been tucked up in bed at the time, while the rest of them were downstairs, watching television.

As soon as the storm had hit, Clay had glanced outside with a frown before telling them he was going to check on Lila. Gavin hadn't paid much attention until Clay had come downstairs, his face worried, unable to find the little girl.

They'd turned the house upside down looking for her, until Gavin had found her huddled in a closet, clasping Tubby close, her face wet with tears. It had taken a while to find her because she wasn't in her closet. She was in Clay's.

It was where she'd felt safest. Not this time, though, this time she'd fallen asleep in their arms.

"Do you think she often hid in a closet as a child?" Colin asked quietly.

Gavin stilled. He didn't want to think about that, about the terror and fear she'd faced as a child before she'd come to them.

"Thank God she didn't hide in a closet that night we found her," Trace said.

Gavin nodded, knowing what he meant. A sweet trick of fate had led them to her that night and if she hadn't been there, if they had never met her... God, he didn't want to even think about it.

Instead he kissed her shoulder and sent a prayer to God, something he rarely did, thanking Him for sending her to them.

Lila woke slowly, yawning, feeling warm and toasty, even if she was lying on something hard that kept moving. Blushing wildly, she gasped as she realized she was lying on someone. Looking up, her gaze connected with Trace's amused one.

"Morning, baby," he rumbled.

The bed shifted and she turned her head to see Gavin staring at her. Those gray eyes studied her before he leaned forward and he kissed her.

"Morning, precious."

A tug on her hair had her turning the other way to look at a sleepy-eyed Colin. "Good morning, Lila." He kissed her.

She cleared her throat. "Wow, a girl, could get used to waking up like this."

"I'm glad you say that," Trace told her. "Because I for one would be glad to wake up like this every day."

She wriggled then stilled as she felt the hard erection poking into her stomach. Her gaze caught Trace's again as she blushed wildly. Chuckling, he ran his hand over her hair. "That's my normal state around you, Lila. I bet it'll be cold showers all round this morning."

The others nodded, groaning.

Lila blushed then moved back so she kneeled between Trace's open legs. She pulled the covers back with her, revealing the three of them to her gaze.

Three delicious, gorgeous men. Gavin lay to her left. Thick

muscles bunched as he raised his arms to place his hands behind his head. His biceps were so thick she doubted she'd be able to get her hands all the way around them.

Her gaze drifted down, over his light sprinkling of chest hair to where his boxers tented with an impressive erection. Lila gulped, clenching her hands into fists to stop herself from pulling his underwear down. His gray eyes were serious, intent as he studied her.

She moved her gaze over to Trace whose green eyes were filled with hunger as he watched her. He had a leaner build, like a swimmer, with narrow hips and wide shoulders.

Finally, she glanced over at Colin. His chest was completely bare of hair, tanned and smooth. He could have been a Californian beach boy. His blond hair lay messily around his head as he cupped his erection, just watching her as he brushed his hand up and down his shaft through his boxers.

"Goddamn you're gorgeous, Lila," Colin groaned.

She glanced down at herself. She was covered in a large T-shirt of Gavin's she'd stolen. She hadn't brushed her hair and she had no make-up on.

And yet they were looking at her like she was the sexiest thing they'd ever seen.

"God damn it," Gavin said, rolling from the bed. "The longer I'm here in this bed with you the harder it gets not to touch you."

Colin nodded and climbed out of bed. "I think I need to go find one of those cold showers."

"Me too," she said ruefully.

Lila raced for the ringing phone.

"Hello," she said breathlessly. No answer, but she could hear someone breathing. "Hello?" Get lost, jerk." This was the third time this week she'd answered the phone to hear a breather on the other end. It was starting to get more than annoying. Rubbing her forehead Lila walked outside to sit by the pool, staring at the glistening water. She couldn't believe that it had been nearly two months since Trace and Colin had knocked on her apartment door. She'd gone from feeling lonely and in despair of her future, to actually looking forward to what was coming next.

And it was all due to Gavin, Trace and Colin. They'd been here for her, holding her when she felt sad over Clay's death, laughing with her, helping her.

They'd made sure that as well as spending time together that each one of them spent time alone with her. Each of them had taken her on a special date this week. Gavin had taken her out for a romantic dinner then a movie. Trace had surprised her with dinner under the stars. Colin had taken her out dancing.

And with each day that passed she fell more in love, and grew more and more attracted to them. They touched her often, caressing her, holding her hand, kissing her. She felt so on fire for them and they had yet to take that last step.

Lila had finally figured out that she had to make the first move. She just needed to work out how and when. She probably needed to get something sexier to wear than her selection of oversized T-shirts. A trip to the spa wouldn't hurt either. The only issue would be paying for it.

Her inheritance hadn't come through yet. She'd been helping Gavin with the bookwork, which worked out well for both of them, but she wasn't about to let him pay her, not when they were paying for everything else.

She hadn't realized how much she'd missed being on the ranch until she'd come back. She'd even dragged out her old cowboy hat; one that Clay had given her years ago.

Oh well, she had a bit of money left, she guessed she could use that.

The phone in the house rang then and she groaned. Not again. She needed to get a whistle or something. Anger pumping through her, she jumped up, racing inside to get it.

"Listen to me, asshole, I'm going to give you one warning—"

"Whoa, what did I do?" a familiar voice asked.

"Laken?" she asked with surprise.

"Yep, you okay?"

"Ah, yeah, sorry," Lila said, blowing a breath out. "Did you try to call me before?"

"No, are you sure you're okay?"

"Yeah, I am," Lila reassured her.

"So girlfriend, are you ready for a night out on the town?"

Lila squealed down the phone as she heard her best friend. "You're home? I can't believe you're here. Why didn't you tell me you were coming back?"

"Yeah, well, my dads are always telling me I don't visit enough, and I was getting a bit tired of New York so I hopped on a plane and here I am."

There was an undercurrent of unhappiness in her friend's voice that had Lila immediately worried. She knew that Laken had been feeling a bit lonely lately, but now she sounded downright sad and dejected. Very unusual for her normally upbeat, self-assured friend.

"And now that I'm home, I'm determined that you and me are going to hit the town."

Lila burst into laughter. "Have you forgotten that there are two bars in town and we're only allowed in one of them?"

Saxon's was a private club that was open to members only and neither Lila nor Laken were members.

"Oh well, we'll hit Dirty Delights and have a blast like old times. Come on, what do you say? Saturday night will be girl's night out."

Lila bit her lip. A girl's night out did sound great and she'd missed Laken horribly.

"Sounds like a plan," she said. "And how about we hit the spa first? Hey, do you mind if I invite someone?"

Max and Logan had brought their wife, Savannah, around for dinner a few nights ago. She and Lila had hit it off instantly. Lila knew that Savannah didn't know many people.

"As long as they don't have a penis, I don't mind," Laken replied. "And the spa sounds like a good plan to me."

The spa was a new thing for Haven. Before, they would have had to have gone into Freestown, but a resort had opened about ten minutes from town and it had a spa that was open to everyone.

"Ooh, are we going to do some men bashing?" Lila asked.

"You betcha. Do you want to make the spa appointments and pick me up? I don't have any transportation at the moment."

"Of course, I'll call right now," Lila promised then hung up.

First, she called Savannah who excitedly agreed to join them then she called the spa and made the necessary appointments. Pleased with herself, she turned her attention to the work waiting for her.

A couple of hours later, she raised her head as a door slammed in the house. What was it with men and not being able to shut doors quietly?

"Baby girl?" Gavin called out.

Lila jumped up and ran out, nearly colliding with him in the hallway.

"Whoa," he said with a laugh, grabbing her and lifting her up against his chest. She held on tight, pressing kisses all over his face. "If I'd known I would get that sort of greeting I'd be home for lunch every day."

"I wouldn't complain," she told him with a laugh. She took his lips with a deep kiss, playing, teasing. His hand crept beneath her skirt, massaging her buttocks.

She moaned. Damn, she needed them soon.

"Hungry, baby girl?"

"Oh yes," she purred. But not for food.

Gavin carried her towards the kitchen as she nibbled on his neck teasingly.

"Minx," he said, slapping her butt before he set her on the kitchen bench. She sat, swinging her legs as she told him about Laken's phone call and their plans for this weekend.

He handed her a sandwich and they moved over to the table to eat their lunch. Gavin touched her often, running his hand over her head and squeezing her thigh.

"Sounds like the three of you will be having fun," he said.

She sighed. "It's been so long since I saw Laken. She sounds kind of sad at the moment, like she needs cheering up."

"I'm sure you can help her with that," Gavin told her. Finishing his food, he stood and placed his plate in the dishwasher. Coming back he leaned down to kiss her lingeringly on the lips.

"Gavin, have you been getting any funny phone calls?"

He pulled back and frowned at her. "Funny how?"

"I've had few phone calls when no one answers on the other end. I can hear them, but they don't talk."

"How many?" he asked sharply.

"Just a couple," she replied. "At first I thought it was a wrong number or maybe a kid."

"Could be," he mused. "Has anything else been happening?"

"No, nothing other than that horrible woman the other day."

"If it happens again, I want to know."

She nodded.

"I'll see you tonight," he told her, kissing her softly. "Love you."

"Love you, too."

She finished up her work then did some tidying up before settling in to watch some television for a while. The slamming of a door startled her some time later as Trace strode into the house.

"Hey, Lila. Shit, I'm sorry, did I wake you up?" He sat on the coffee table opposite the sofa and pushed a curl off her face. "You okay?"

"No, I was just in a daze. Shoot, is that the time? I was going to start making dinner."

Six p.m.? Crap.

"Don't worry about that, shorty. I'll get something started."

"You guys are the ones who go to work each day," she said, trying to sit up. He pushed her back down gently. "The least I can do is the housework and cooking."

Trace chucked her under the chin. "You don't need to wear yourself to the bone looking after this place. Sure, we appreciate it, don't for one second think we don't. But you are not our house-keeper, understand?"

"But I owe you so much and I contribute so little." At least once the money came through from her inheritance she'd be able to help out with the bills. "Once my money comes through I will pay you all back."

"Pay us back for what?" Trace asked in a low voice. That should have warned her she was skating on thin ice, but she wasn't paying close enough attention.

"For all the food and bills and stuff.".

"Lila Stacia Richards you will not be giving us any of your money, do you understand me?" he asked in a hard voice. She jumped, not used to hearing that tone from Trace.

She sat up and this time he let her. "Oh yes, I will. I pay my own way."

"You will not," he stated emphatically. "You try to give any of us money and your ass will be so red you won't sit for a week!"

Her jaw dropped at that statement as she stared at him in shock. "That's hardly fair. I wanted to do something nice and you threaten spank me!"

"Oh, it's no threat. It's a promise. Try to give us any money and your butt will be on fire."

"No way." Standing, she faced him, her hands on her hips. "I am not letting you get away with bullying me like that. You can only spank me if I risk myself or my safety, you don't get to spank me for doing the right thing."

He stood, scowling. "Are you trying to insult us by insinuating that we can't take care of you?"

She gaped at him, her jaw dropping open. "Of course not, you idiot."

"Good. That's that. You will not be giving us any of your money and that's final."

Lila just shook her head in frustration as he walked off.

Men. And they said women were hard to understand?

9

"Got your phone, Lila?" Colin asked as he pulled up outside Dirty Delights, the name didn't really match the rustic outside. But there was always a good band playing on a Saturday night and already it was pumping.

She'd spent the morning getting massaged, waxed and pampered at the spa with Savannah and Laken, who had hit it off straight away. It had put a dint in her credit card but it had all been worth it.

"Yep, and it's fully charged, Dad," she teased him.

"Cheeky brat. Okay, so call when you want to come home and then wait inside, I'll come get you. Understand?"

This was only like the fourth time she'd heard this. And that was only on the ride in.

"You know, I can take care of myself, Colin. I lived in Phoenix all by myself. I'm a big girl."

"But you're our girl, now," he told her, his gaze softening as he pushed a curl behind her ear. "And we enjoy taking care of you. We just want to make sure you're safe."

Her insides softened at his words.

"I know," she replied. "And I'm so glad that you do. But I promise I will be careful. I have my phone, I have my purse, and I will call you when I want to leave. I will stay with Savannah and Laken. Scout's honor. This is Haven, remember? It's not like we can really get into any trouble."

Colin chuckled. "I'm not so sure, you girls could find trouble anywhere. Come on, I'll walk you in. Oh, by the way," he reached into his pocket and pulled out some cash, "this is from Gavin. Your money for all the work you've been doing."

Lila shook her head. "No way, I'm not taking any money off you guys."

Colin's gaze narrowed. "You earned it. Either you take it or I'll just go on in and tell Joe to add it on a tab for you and not let you pay for any drinks."

She knew he would too. With a sigh and a shake of her head, she took the cash, tucking it carefully into her purse.

With a grin, she rolled her eyes when he turned his back. He was just lucky he was so adorable.

Lila threw her arms up, dancing with abandon, sandwiched between Laken and Savannah. Dirty Delights was packed tonight, a rodeo in the next town over had brought a number of visitors in. Unfortunately, some of their manners weren't as good as the locals.

She gritted her teeth as she felt another pinch on her ass.

Patience. Patience.

She kept dancing, feeling a bit light-headed. She probably shouldn't have had that fifth or was it sixth vodka and orange?

A hand smacked her heavily on the ass. Oh no. That was just too much. Turning, she found a rather attractive cowboy smiling at her. With a grin of her own that would have had her men immediately backing off, she reached around and slapped him on the ass.

His smile immediately grew. Damn it. Dumb, drunken ass.

"Back off, idiot," she told him, turning back to her friends. An arm crept around her waist, hauling her backward.

"Let me go!" she yelled, her voice barely making audible over the noise of the music. She kicked back, pulling at his arm. Laken leaped forward, shoving the guy back. He let go of her and Lila stepped forward, whirling around to confront him. But Laken was already there, right in his face.

"Get lost, jerk," Laken growled.

The cowboy glared down at them, a sullen look on his face. Uh-oh, this could turn bad. Very bad.

"There a problem here?" a new voice asked.

Lila looked up to see Duncan Jones staring down at them, his face calm even though his eyes were intent and focused on Laken.

Laken and Duncan stared at one another with enough heat to set the room aflame.

"Hey, I got no problem, buddy. Just looking for a dance," the cowboy said quickly.

Well, he can't have been too drunk, because he still had some sense. Of course, Duncan was pretty intimidating. He was built, really built with muscles that didn't quit.

"Good," Duncan said, having no problem making himself heard over the music. "I suggest you go look elsewhere and this time, keep your hands to yourself."

The cowboy scurried off.

"Thanks, Duncan," Lila said with a smile.

Duncan smiled gently down at her. "No problem."

"Don't thank him," Laken said hotly. "We were doing just fine without him."

Lila looked over at Laken in surprise. Laken could be fiery and tough, but she wasn't rude. Duncan raised a brow, a quelling look in his eyes. Lila's butt clenched. She knew that look. If it had been one of her men giving her that look then her butt would be in a world of trouble.

"That so, Laken?" Duncan drawled, crossing his arms over his wide chest. "And what if that cowboy's buddies had decided to join him, were you going to take care of them too? All five-foot-two of you?"

Laken straightened her shoulders. "Actually, I'm five feet three and we would have been fine. We can take care of ourselves. No one asked for your help, so why don't you run on back to wherever you crawled out of?"

"Laken!" Lila scolded as Savannah watched on, her eyes wide.

"Too far, little girl, too far." Duncan took a step forward and Laken blanched but stood her ground.

Lila quickly stepped between them. "Duncan, can I buy you a drink to say thanks?"

Duncan's dark gaze shifted to her and softened. "No thanks, squirt. Is Gavin here tonight? I haven't seen him."

"No, we're on a girl's night. You know what, I kind of feel like sitting down for a while. Good to see you again, Duncan, and thanks."

Grabbing hold of Laken and Savannah, she dragged them behind her, actually managing to find a free table. She moved the glasses and bottles to one side before sitting with a sigh.

"Damn that man. He's such a fucking asshole," Laken said as she sat down.

"Duncan? What do you have against him?" Lila asked. "He's always been really nice to me and he's a good friend of Gavin's."

"He's a jerk," Laken said emphatically. "A bossy, know-it-all, Neanderthal jerk."

Savannah and Lila looked at each other.

"I don't know him well," Savannah said. "But he once stopped to help me when I got a flat tire. I was in the middle of changing it when he pulled up, changed it for me then took my flat one into the garage in town. Of course, he also scolded me the whole time for not calling Logan and Max. They were on round-up and busy. But not too busy for Logan to meet me at home and, well..." she shifted uncomfortably on the chair.

Lila smiled sympathetically while Laken glared. "See, he's a tattletale as well as a bossy jerk. How dare he tell on you to Logan and scold you. Who does he think he is?"

Savannah shrugged. "I don't know, I've lived in the city where no one really gave a hoot if I was safe or not. I used to walk around the streets late at night, drive too fast, and forget to lock my door. It's quite nice living here, in a place where the men take care of women, look out for them—"

"Treat them like children, tell them what to do, spank them," Laken finished.

Lila sighed, really worried about her friend. She seemed so bitter.

Reaching over, Lila grabbed her hand, shocked to see tears well in her friend's eyes. "Oh, baby, what happened? This isn't you? Why have you come home? Why are you so angry?"

"Because everything is ruined," Laken spat out. "My career, my relationship. I was doing so well, I had a great job, friends, and the perfect boyfriend."

"Ricky?" Lila asked. She'd never met him, but Laken had spoken about him like he was marvelous.

"He was gorgeous and so sweet and he didn't try to tell me what to do, he let me have my space. We'd just meet up at parties or for dinner but we both led our own lives. You know? No pressure."

Lila thought that sounded like they were friends with benefits rather than in a relationship.

"What happened?" she asked.

Laken glanced up, misery in her eyes. "He cheated on me. I

found him with my assistant. Even worse than that, he got me fired. His father owned the company. Ricky and my assistant claimed that I had been bullying her. I got fired."

"Oh God, honey, I'm so sorry." Lila drew her close, hugging her tightly.

"I feel so stupid. I had to come home to my dads because I have no savings, I couldn't afford my rent. I couldn't even afford food. I'm broke, homeless and jobless. I had to borrow money to come here tonight. Could things get any worse?" she wailed.

Lila and Savannah cuddled in close to her. A waitress dressed in a tight top Lila had ever seen came over with an empty tray to clear their table. Her hair was a dark brown and pulled back into a ponytail that hung down her back.

She didn't say a word, just started picking up the glasses and bottles.

"Thanks," Lila said with a smile as the woman picked up a half-empty bottle of beer. The waitress turned, a look of venom on her face.

"No worries," she snarled then tipped the bottle straight onto Lila's lap.

"Aww," Lila cried out, quickly standing and shaking out her dress.

"Hey, what are you doing, bitch?" Laken yelled, standing and leaning over the table as though she were going to push the waitress away. Savannah reached into her purse and pulled out some tissues, dabbing at the wet stain ineffectively.

"Laken, it's okay, just some beer," Lila tried to soothe her friend who she knew was more than capable of starting a bar brawl. It wouldn't be the first time.

"Yeah, ahh, sorry, it was an accident," the waitress said, not looking one bit apologetic as she scampered away.

"Accident my ass," Laken said, taking a step as though to follow. Lila reached out and grabbed her arm. "Laken, don't worry.

It doesn't matter. I think I'm done for the night, though. I'll just go tidy up in the bathroom and call Colin. He said he'd take us all home."

Savannah nodded. "I'm getting tired. I'm more than ready to go home."

Laken agreed somewhat reluctantly.

"Wait here, guys," Lila said. "I'll be back soon."

She moved through the crowd to the bathroom as fast as she could. A woman left as Lila entered. Turning the tap in the sink on, she tried to wash off the worst of the beer. Sighing, she looked in the mirror, tidying herself up. The door to the bathroom opened. She glanced sideways as an older woman entered and stood beside her, staring at her.

"You're Lila West."

Lila stilled. She hadn't heard that name in a long time. Slowly, she turned to look at the woman. She was only an inch or two taller than Lila herself. Dark hair lay lankly down her back. Her face was lined; her eyes were tired and dull, as though she'd lived a hard life.

"Actually, I'm Lila Richards," she said.

The other woman just stared at her, a decidedly calculated look in her eyes. Lila's stomach dropped. The woman coughed, a hacking, harsh sound that made Lila wince. "Took his name, did you?"

"Who are you?" Lila demanded.

"Why darling, don't you recognize me? I'm so crushed."

Lila's blood ran cold as she stared at the other woman. There was something about her. Those eyes... But that was impossible, wasn't it?

"I'm your mother," the woman replied. "I can't believe you've forgotten your own mother."

Lila stopped breathing, just stared at the other woman in disbelief. Surely not. What would bring her mother here? She lived in Chicago. What the hell would she be doing in Haven, Texas?

"You must be mistaken."

The other woman smiled. It wasn't a friendly look. "Oh, I assure you, I'm not mistaken. My name is Abigail West and I am your mother. I gave birth to you, took care of you for the first seven years of your life until Clay Richards took you away from me."

Dear Lord. Was it actually true? Lila had figured on never seeing this woman again. What was she doing here?

"He didn't take me, you gave me to him," Lila said through numb lips. She had to get out of here, get away from this woman.

It couldn't be a coincidence she was here. She hadn't contacted Lila in all these years so what was she doing here now?

"Why are you here? Did you come looking for me?"

"I'm here because you and that up-himself cowboy owe me," Abigail snarled. "I'm here to collect."

Lila took a step towards her, hands clenched into fists. "Don't you talk about Clay that way, you bitch!"

"Lila? Is everything all right?"

Lila turned to find Savannah standing in the doorway, looking worried. She forced a smile onto her face. "Fine. Sorry I'm taking so long. I'll be right out."

"Sure?" Savannah looked doubtfully over at the woman Abigail.

"I'm sure," Lila said firmly.

"Okay, I'll wait for you right outside," Savannah told her.

As Savannah left, Lila gave the other woman a hard look. "You're the one who called the house the other day. I owe you nothing. I want you to go away and stay away."

"I need money."

"Well, you've come to the wrong person, lady," Lila said, feeling sick at the realization that she was related to this woman. "Because

I don't have any money and even if I did I wouldn't give any to you."

"Now, now, don't lie. From what I heard you're loaded. I know Richards had money and that you're fucking his sons. So you will get me my money one way or another."

"Or what?" Lila said, feeling completely ill at the realization that this woman was her mother.

"Or I will tell everyone I can that your precious cowboy stole my darling daughter. Will people think he's so great then?"

Lila glared at her. "You really think that people around here will believe you?"

"Maybe, maybe not, but just think how quick it would spread far and wide, especially when I tell them that you're fucking his sons. Think people will be so accepting of you all outside of this weird town? People like to talk and they don't like anything out of the ordinary. I think a lot of people would love to hear about how depraved this place is, and when I tell them that Clay Richards brought my only child here and corrupted her, well, we'll just see what they say, won't we?"

"You old bitch." Lila wanted to tell her to fuck off. But she wasn't so sure that Abigail wouldn't do exactly as she promised. And there was no way Lila was going to risk any dirt touching Clay or her men. "What will it take to get rid of you?" she asked through gritted teeth.

"One hundred thousand."

"I can't get my hands on that sort of cash," Lila replied incredulously.

"You will. Meet me on Monday at five at that old church off Branton road."

"There's no way I can get one hundred thousand together by Monday."

"Fine, make it Tuesday. See how reasonable I can be? Five pm. Don't keep me waiting, darling."

Abigail turned and left, leaving Lila shaken and unnerved. The door opened again and she jumped, turning. But it was only Savannah.

"Oh, Lila, I knew something was wrong, you're pale as a ghost." Savannah stepped forward and placed her arm around Lila's shoulders. "What happened? Who was that woman? Do you know her?"

Lila shook her head, holding her hand over her stomach. She felt sick and worried. Not for herself or about the money, but what Abigail might do to her men, to Clay's memory.

"I really want to go home," Lila said.

"Okay, let's get out of here."

Numbly, Lila let Savannah lead her from the bathroom.

COLIN SEASONED THE SCRAMBLED EGGS, knowing they were Lila's favorite. He wondered if he should go check on her. She hadn't seemed drunk last night when he'd picked her up, but perhaps she was feeling a bit worse for wear this morning.

"Lila not up yet?" Trace asked as he walked in.

Colin shook his head. "I was just wondering whether I should get her up."

"I just heard her shower come on," Gavin said as he strode in.

Colin set the table. By the time Lila walked in ten minutes later, he had all the food out and waiting for her. They all sat down together. Everyone dug in except for Lila who looked down at her plate listlessly.

"Have a good night, sweetheart?" Trace asked.

Nodding, she attempted a smile. "It was really good to see Laken, and Savannah too."

"You don't look like you had much sleep," Gavin commented with a frown.

She shrugged and pushed the food around on her plate. The three men looked at each other in worry.

"Do you know when the money comes through from the estate?" she asked suddenly.

"Tomorrow, I think," Colin said. "Did you have enough money last night?"

"Oh, yes, I had plenty with what you gave me." She sent Gavin a frown. "I told you I didn't want you paying me, you guys have already given me too much."

Trace leaned forward. "You better not try to give us any of your money, Lila. I believe we've already had that conversation."

"What conversation?" Colin asked.

Gavin leaned back in his chair, folding his arms. Lila squirmed a bit before stilling and staring back at them all.

"Lila seems to be under the mistaken impression that she owes us," Trace said. "And I told her that if she tried to give us any of her money then I would spank her butt bright red. What she doesn't understand is that we like taking care of her, that it fills something inside us to look after her, protect her, making sure that she has everything she needs."

Lila remained silent, nibbling on her lip.

"Lila?" Gavin questioned. "What's wrong?"

"Nothing's wrong," she told him, sounding uncharacteristically grouchy. This wasn't the Lila they knew and something was wrong. Very wrong.

"Lila, eat your breakfast," Gavin bossed.

"I'm not hungry." She stood, her chair scraping back. "Nothing's wrong. I just don't feel like talking, all right?"

She turned away, but Gavin grabbed her around the waist before she could flee. Ignoring the way she fought, he stood and dragged her against him, her back to his chest.

She sagged against him. Gavin sat and pulled her down onto his lap, rocking her.

All three men looked at each other with worry.

"What's wrong, baby girl?" Gavin crooned to her.

Collin crouched down in front of them. "Did something happen, Lila?"

She buried her face against Gavin's chest.

"Little one," Colin said. "We just want to help you. Tell us what's going on. Please." He couldn't stand seeing her like this. "Did something happen last night?"

She shook her head. Everyone remained silent for a long moment before Colin sighed and ran his hand over her back. "Want to lie on the couch and watch a movie, Lila?"

Lila nodded and he scooped her up, carrying her down to the living room and settling her on the couch. He lifted her head then sat, settling her head on his lap so he could rub her temples.

Switching on the TV, he turned it down low. They sat there silently for a long time. Gavin and Trace popped in from time to time. About an hour after he'd settled them in, he glanced down to find her fast asleep.

What the hell happened last night?

Trace stepped into the room, sitting on the coffee table as he stared down at Lila, a look of love and concern on his face. Colin knew how Trace felt, he couldn't imagine his life without her now. He couldn't believe that he'd almost pushed her away.

Trace sighed. "Duncan just called. Said he had to chase some cowboy away from the girls last night. Apparently, there were a few strangers in town because of the rodeo in Freestown. Duncan reckoned Laken was about to have the guy's balls. Think that could be the problem?"

Colin frowned. "Maybe. Did Duncan say if she seemed upset?" He wondered why the other man didn't call them straight away.

Trace shook his head. "No, he reckoned they were fine. Laken was plenty angry, but he said Lila was calming the situation down. Said he would have called us if he thought there was a problem."

"Next time they want a girl's night one of us will be going to watch over them," Gavin said emphatically from the doorway.

"They're not going to like that," Trace warned, ever the peacemaker.

Gavin shrugged his shoulders. "Their safety comes first."

"They had people looking out for them," Colin said. "But I'd rather one of us had been there, even if we'd just watched over them from afar. Then we might have some idea of what is wrong with Lila this morning. I don't like seeing her like this. She seems dejected. Maybe Savannah can shed some light on things." Colin shifted Lila's head off his lap. "I'll go talk to her. I've wanted to talk to Max about a hunting trip anyway."

"Savi, you still in bed, darlin'?" Logan called out.

Savannah groaned and opened one eye to look at him. "Not so loud," she told him in a whisper as he lay down on the bed with her.

He grinned. It amazed her how she could make this big, serious bear of a man happy. But every time he smiled a little thrill went through her.

"Had a bit too much to drink, huh, Savi girl?"

She winced. Damn man didn't have volume control. "Yes. And I would really like to be left alone to wallow in self-pity."

"No can do, darlin'. Colin's coming over and he wants to talk to you."

She opened her other eye. "He's coming to talk to me?"

"Apparently there's something wrong with Lila and she's not talking to them, they're hoping you can help them understand what went on last night."

Savannah frowned. "We had a good time last night. I mean,

there was a cowboy with loose hands but Duncan Jones helped us out with that."

"Who touched you?" Logan asked with a growl. He stood, looking ready to hunt them down and beat them to a pulp. Savannah smiled, completely taken with his protectiveness.

"Relax, honey, he's long gone and I wouldn't be able to point him out to you even if I did come across him."

Logan scowled then waggled his finger at her. "That's the last time you go out without Max or me running interference."

"It was a girl's night out, Logan, I can hardly bring one of you along to play bodyguard."

"I happen to make a very good bodyguard," Max said as he entered with a smile. "You wouldn't even notice I was there."

Savannah scowled then winced as even that small movement seemed to make her headache worse.

"Colin just pulled up, love," Max told her. "Why don't you get ready and join us downstairs?"

Savannah rose as they left, holding her head with her hands. She spotted a glass of water and some painkillers on the bed.

"Logan, bless you," she said. He might be quiet and a bit over-protective but he was also the most thoughtful man she'd ever met.

Taking the painkillers, she gulped down the water and moved into the bathroom to take a quick shower.

I should not have had those last two or three shots.

Fifteen minutes later, feeling a lot better than she had before, she moved slowly down the stairs to join the men in the living room.

"Hey, Savannah," Colin greeted, leaning over to peck her on the cheek. She sat between Max and Logan on the couch.

"Hi, Colin. The guys said you came over to see me?" Colin was a gorgeous man. He had nothing on her two men, of course, but he was definitely a hunk with his deep brown eyes and that blond, shaggy hair.

Colin nodded, his face more serious than she'd ever seen it. "Yes, honey, I just wanted to see if anything happened last night that would upset Lila."

Savannah frowned. She didn't want to betray Lila by bringing up something she obviously didn't want to share. There was only one moment during the night when Lila had seemed truly upset.

That woman Lila had been talking with seemed off. Savannah had met her fair share of bad people. And that woman had wrong written all over her.

"Savi," Max said warningly, his eyes narrowing as he stared at her. "It's obvious something happened."

Savannah stared back at him. She would not be bullied. He gave her that look which meant he was not backing down and unless she did her butt was toast.

She just snorted.

Colin's lips twitched, obviously knowing exactly what was going on between them. "I think she just imagined giving you the finger, my friend," he said to Max.

"Hmm." Max sat back and crossed his arms. Logan just watched, but that was Logan, he'd remain quiet unless he had something important to add.

"Hey," she said, glowering at Colin. "I thought you wanted my help."

"Sorry." Colin gave her a sheepish smile. "Please, Savannah."

"Lila's my friend," she told him, agonizing over what to do.

"And I don't want you to betray her trust," Colin told her earnestly. "But this is something the old Lila would do, shut herself down to hide any problems or hurts and it can be destructive. If you can help us in any way we'd be grateful. We're worried about her. I haven't seen her so depressed before, not even when Clay died."

Savannah felt a stab of worry. "Well, we had a good time last night, right up until the end. Some cowboy slapped Lila's ass," she saw Colin's eyes narrow and went on quickly, "but she took care of him, and Duncan Jones was there. He quickly got rid of the guy. After that we went back to the table and had a talk. Mainly about some stuff that Laken went through with her job and her ex. Then some waitress spilled a drink on Lila so she went to clean up in the bathroom. I followed her after I realized she was taking quite a while. When I walked in she was talking to a woman." Savannah paused, wondering how much she should say.

"Please, Savannah," Colin begged.

With a sigh, Savannah hoped she wasn't about to lose a friend, but she just knew she couldn't keep this to herself. "Well, I didn't recognize the woman, and I didn't hear what they were saying, but Lila seemed kind of upset. I'm not sure exactly what they were speaking about, but I'm guessing she might have something to do with Lila acting strange today."

Colin sighed and gave her a smile. "Thanks, Savannah, I owe you."

Savannah nodded and stood with her men as Colin went to leave. "I really like Lila, I hope everything is okay."

"It will be. It will be."

LILA LAY ON HER BED, staring up at the ceiling. She knew she should tell her men about last night. She'd promised to be honest with them and they wouldn't be happy if she met her mother on Tuesday alone.

But she just couldn't bring herself to tell them what her mother had threatened. Shame washed through her. How could she be related to someone so awful? And what if Gavin, Trace and Colin were so disgusted that they turned away from her? She wouldn't blame them, but it would break her.

She let out a loud sigh. She'd retreated to her bedroom to think and yet that was the last thing she wanted to do. She wanted her men to hug her, touch her, to make love to her. Lila squeezed her eyes shut as her body heated, her nipples tightening.

She was ready for them. Rolling her nipple between her forefinger and thumb, she groaned as sensation raced through her body to sizzle around her clit.

"Lila?" Trace called through the door, knocking gently. "Are you okay in there?"

She stilled, staring at the closed door. Did she dare?

Moving her free hand up to her other nipple, she licked her bottom lip. Yep, seemed she did.

"Come in," she called huskily.

Trace stepped through the door and came to a sudden stop. The concern and determination on his face faded to be replaced by a hot, intense heat.

"What." He cleared his throat, his gaze riveted on her breasts. "What are you doing?"

"Trying to relieve some pressure," she replied. "Want to help me?"

He took a step forward then another before stopping at the foot of the bed. Lila split her legs, hardly believing her own daring. Dropping one hand down, she lifted her skirt and cupped her mound.

Trace's breathing quickened, a light flush covering his face. "This isn't a good idea, you're not ready."

"Do I look like I'm not ready, Trace?" she asked in a low voice as she slipped one finger beneath her lacy panties.

"Colin just pulled up... What the hell?" Gavin asked.

Lila glanced over at Gavin who'd come to a stop just inside her bedroom. She smiled, hoping it looked inviting rather than nervous. Although since she'd started her nerves had pretty much fled. This seemed so right.

"What are you doing?" Gavin asked, shaking himself free of his shock as he came to stand by Trace.

"I need you guys," she told them. "So much. I can't wait anymore, don't make me wait anymore. Touch me. Help me."

Both men's eyes widened and she glanced down their bodies, taking in the heavy erections pressing against their jeans. Oh yeah, they wanted this. Badly.

"You sure about this?" Gavin asked.

She nodded.

"Hey, Lila, we need to have a talk... Oh, what the hell have I been missing out on?" Colin didn't hesitate, just walked straight towards them, his gaze on her breasts.

"Nothing yet," she told him. "Although I have a neglected nipple that needs your touch."

"Baby, I thought you'd never ask." He dropped down to his knees and raised her tight T-shirt, revealing her bra. She should have known Colin wouldn't take any convincing. As though his readiness to dive straight in helped eliminate their hesitance, Trace and Gavin moved, stripping as Colin pulled her clothes off then moved on to his own.

Lila gulped, looking at three hard, gorgeous bodies.

Yum.

10

"Damn, you are hot," Gavin told her.

"So beautiful, I can't wait to touch you, lick you all over, taste you," Colin said.

Trace just smiled.

She sighed. She was on fire, her whole body one giant nerve-ending. She needed them now.

"Open your legs wider, baby," Gavin growled, standing at the base of the bed. Trace nipped his way down her neck as Colin kissed over her stomach. She kept her gaze on Gavin, though, his gray eyes intense, hot.

She slowly moved her thighs apart. Immediately, Gavin's gaze dropped to her moist folds as Colin and Trace lavished attention on her nipples. They each hooked an arm beneath one of her legs and pulled them up, splitting her wide.

Lila whimpered and closed her eyes, knowing exactly how exposed she was.

"No hiding," Gavin ordered. "Look at me."

Colin bit a nipple in punishment as Trace just kept lapping at her, seemingly caught up in his play.

She opened her eyes and stared up at Gavin as he ran his hand up and down his impressive erection. "You sure you're ready for this?" he asked. "We do this now and there is no going back. We will take you wherever and whenever we need you. There will be no holding back from us."

Possessive intent lit his eyes. She nodded. "I'm ready."

He knelt between her legs, his fingers parting her. He just stared at her for a moment.

"Fuck, yeah." He dropped his mouth to her pussy, running his tongue lightly over her clit.

"Gavin!"

Electrical shocks filled her body and she thrust her hips up. She needed more. Need to come. He thrust one finger deep, moving it too slowly in and out of her. Time and time again, he brought her to the edge of coming then pulled back. Trace and Colin were no better, playing with her breasts, kissing her incessantly until she was a writhing mass of sensation.

"Please, please, please." Her breaths had become harsh sobs, her body so in need she could barely stand it.

Then Gavin drew back and reached over to grab the condom Trace handed him.

"You don't need it," she said breathlessly. "I'm on the Pill. I'm clean."

He paused then his gaze narrowed. He smiled. "I've never taken a woman without one." He threw it away. "You're my first."

She liked the sound of that. Trace took her mouth in a deep kiss as Gavin started pushing his way inside her. Inch by agonizing inch, slowly he penetrated her until she was full.

Trace pulled back and she reached down to grasp his hard cock. He groaned. "Jesus, your touch feels so good."

"Gavin, Gavin, please, I can't stand it!" she screamed. He paused, not moving, just holding himself inside her.

"Please what?" he asked.

"Move, I need you to move."

"Your wish is my command, baby girl."

And then he was moving against her, within her, making her shudder. Colin and Trace soothed her, holding her tight. Gavin's thrusts grew faster. That knot inside her tightened and she screamed as Gavin thrust her up and over into bliss. It slammed into her, robbing her of her breath, so intense she swore she saw stars. His own yell of satisfaction barely penetrated as she shook her way through the orgasm.

She came to with a shudder, deep breaths sawing in and out of her lungs. Gavin rolled to her side, drawing her in close, he held her against his chest as she drifted down from that orgasm.

"Okay, baby?" Gavin asked her.

"More than okay, wonderful, amazing."

Grinning, he ran his hand over her body. "Think you're up for more?" Gavin nodded down at Colin who was kissing his way up her leg. She smiled. Sure, she was still languishing in the glow of a fantastic orgasm. But who wouldn't want more?

"Oh yeah," she replied.

Suddenly, she was rolled over and placed on her hands and knees as Trace sat up against the headboard. Her head rested close to his lap as Colin spread her legs wide. Trace grasped the base of his cock, his hand holding it tightly.

"Open up, baby," Gavin ordered.

With a grin, she eagerly did just that, taking Trace into her mouth, humming with delight. She bobbed her head, moving slow then fast as Trace ran his hands over her head. She licked her way down his cock, loving the silken feel of him, getting to know each inch.

"So good, Lila, that feels like heaven."

Colin pushed his way inside her with one firm thrust, filling her so completely that she stilled for a moment, just delighting in the sensation. Then he pulled back and pressed forward.

"Keep sucking, Lila, take me deep," Trace told her. She turned her attention back to Trace, although it was hard to concentrate, especially when Gavin dipped his hand beneath her stomach to play with her clit.

Colin continued her steady rhythm and she felt her body tightening once more. She sucked hard on Trace's cock, determined to give them as much pleasure as they gave her.

"I'm coming, Lila. Pull back if you need to," Trace warned.

Pull back? Was he mad?

Lila swallowed, taking him deep as he came. Colin moved faster, coming loudly, triggering her own release as Gavin continued to tap at her clit, drawing her release out, making her shudder with each wave of bliss.

"What did you learn from Savannah?" Gavin asked half an hour later. Lila lay on Trace, her head resting against his chest. Gavin and Colin lay on either side, surrounding her. She didn't care what they were talking about; they had just sent her to heaven. Multiple times. And she really had no interest in anything but lying here and dozing.

Colin sighed. "That our girl is keeping something from us." His hand grasped her bottom and squeezed.

"Hey!" she cried out.

"We need to have a little chat about what happened last night."

She stiffened and Trace ran his hand down her back in an attempt to soothe her. "Easy, Lila, just talk to us."

"And if I'm not ready to talk?"

"You just gave yourself to us," Gavin stated. "You'll talk."

"This is what being in a relationship is," Colin added. "Sharing with us, talking to us. Let us in."

Gavin rubbed her bottom, stirring her interest once again.

Trace's cock grew against her stomach and she sighed. Would she ever get enough of them?

Lord, she hoped not.

"Who was the woman you were talking to last night?" Colin asked.

Lila stilled. How did he know about that? "What did Savannah tell you?" Remembering what they'd said before.

"What she did or didn't say doesn't matter, does it, baby girl?" Gavin asked, still teasing her. "Because you're going to tell us, aren't you?"

She turned her head to stare at him. "If I tell you I'm afraid you won't want me anymore."

Gavin sat and pulled her off Trace to sit on his lap, holding her against him tightly. He kissed the top of her head. Trace and Colin sat up, watching her, their hands running over her soothingly.

"Nothing you said could make us reject you. You're our whole world," Gavin told her.

"What is it?" Trace asked her. "Tell us and we'll do whatever we can to help."

"It-it's my mother."

GAVIN JOLTED IN SHOCK. Out of everything he'd possibly expected to come from her mouth, this hadn't entered his mind. "Your mother?"

Lila shook and he held her closer, wishing he could take away all her fear and pain.

"You've seen your mother?" Trace asked gently.

Lila sat up. "She was at Dirty Delights last night. I didn't even realize who she was at first. I didn't recognize her. She, oh God, she's so awful."

"What did she do?" Colin asked as he looked at his brothers in concern.

"She-she threatened to tell everyone that Clay stole me and about how the four of us live together. She said she would spread nasty rumors, make your lives hell, painting Clay as a child kidnapper."

"Oh, baby," Gavin said. "Let her do her worst. We don't care what she says. Everyone who knows Clay will know that wasn't true."

"But how dare she try to make out that Clay was the bad guy! He rescued me. He wanted me when she didn't give a shit. And I don't want her spreading nasty rumors about you guys. I can't believe I'm related to her!"

"Neither can we, Lila," Colin told her. "You're beautiful, kind and generous. She is nothing like you."

"She's my mother, though, what if I end up like her?" Lila wailed. "How can you want to be with me when I'm related to her?"

Gavin shook his head. He couldn't believe she was actually worried about ending up like that bitch. "Baby girl, there is no way you could ever end up like her. I promise. She may have given birth to you, but Clay raised you and he raised you right."

She finally relaxed a bit and he knew she was listening.

"But what if people turn on you like they did with Colin after Sara spread her bile around?" She kept her gaze down, not looking at any of them.

"Oh, baby," Colin breathed, kneeling before her. "Look at me, Lila." He waited until she turned to look up at him. "No matter what this bitch does I would never blame you. I was a different guy back then, I didn't have all of you backing me up. Let her do her worst. I'm ready."

"What does she gain by spreading rumors, though?" Gavin asked with a frown and Lila immediately stiffened again.

"Lila?" Trace asked. "That wasn't everything, was it?"

She shook her head. "No. She wants money. She said if I gave her one hundred thousand she'd keep quiet."

"And you were going to give it to her, weren't you?" Anger lashed through Gavin at what her mother was doing to her own daughter. Worst of all Lila hadn't come and told them straight away. "That's why you wanted to know when the money from Clay was coming through? You were actually going to pay her off? How? Did she seriously expect you to withdraw it and hand it over in a suitcase?"

Lila winced. "Umm. I'm supposed to meet her at the old church on the Banning's ranch. She mentioned something about a bank transfer."

"Let me get this straight," Gavin said quietly. "You were going to meet this woman to give her a hundred grand by yourself, without telling us?"

Guilt crossed her face and he knew she had been planning on doing just that. Fury raced through him, nearly blinding him. Thinking of what could have happened to her literally had him shaking.

"Yes."

Gavin stood and started pacing up and down. God damn it, he was tired of her putting herself at risk. What would it take to get her to fully trust them? To know that they were going nowhere, that they would never abandon her no matter what.

"G-Gavin?" she said tremulously. She was huddled on the bed, curled in on herself, her eyes wide as she watched him. Trace and Colin were staring at her in concern, trying to soothe her, but her eyes were set on him.

There was worry there. And no small amount of guilt. God, it hurt that she still didn't trust them enough to confide in them, to let them help her. But he couldn't force trust. It would come, he just had to be patient and look out for her until she learned that she could come to them with anything.

Gavin held his hand out to her. "Come here."

She jumped up and raced towards him. He pulled her into his arms, placing kisses over her head.

"You terrify me at times, you really do. The idea of you meeting with that bitch alone terrifies me. But no matter what I love you, got me?"

Gavin held her back, his hands on her shoulders as he shook her lightly.

She nodded. "She's so awful. She was the one who called that day and I suppose she's behind the hang-ups we've been getting. I just can't believe I'm related to her."

"Shh, honey, it's okay. You are nothing like her. I promise." He held her close, running his hand up and down her back. "How about if Trace runs you a bath? I think you could use a bit of pampering."

He nodded at Trace who climbed from the bed and moved into the adjoining bathroom.

"Everything is going to be all right," Gavin reassured her. "As long as we're together it will be okay."

LILA FELT GUILTY. So horrible that she couldn't stand it. She'd hurt them. Really hurt them. She should have told them. She knew she should have, but she couldn't bear for them to know how awful her mother was. To have them regret being with her.

The disappointment and hurt in their faces broke her heart, though.

A loud knock surprised her and she glanced over at her bathroom door. She sat up a bit in the bath, only now noticing how cold it had grown.

"Yes?" she called out.

"You okay in there, Lila?" Trace asked. "You've been in there for an hour now."

She had?

"I'm just getting out now." Would he ask her if she needed help?

"Okay, we're down in the living room."

She heard him move away and her stomach dropped. Slowly, she climbed out of the tub, feeling like an old woman. Her body ached from their lovemaking, but that was a pleasant sort of pain. The rest of her felt drained, emotionally done in.

Lila grabbed some sweatpants and a long T-shirt. She moved down the stairs, her stomach tied into knots. There was still a part of her that expected them to walk away from her, to realize they could do so much better.

Walking into the living room, she stared over at the three of them. Gavin was leaning against the mantelpiece, his arms folded across his thick chest as he stared down at the floor. Colin lay sprawled on the sofa, a beer in his hand.

Two arms slid around her waist from behind, pulling her against his wide chest. She let out a gasp of fright.

"Jesus, Trace, you scared me."

He chuckled, nuzzling her neck. "Sorry, you seemed like you could use a hug. You okay?"

Lila looked over at Colin and Gavin who were staring over at her. She shrugged.

Trace bit her neck lightly, a clear reprimand. "Talk to us."

"I just...you're all staring at me like I did something wrong when I only did what each one of you would have. I tried to protect you." How come it was okay for them to protect her but when she tried to do the same they got all upset?

Gavin shook his head in disappointment. "No, honey, you didn't do what the rest of us would have done."

"Are you saying that you wouldn't have tried to protect me if someone was threatening me? Come on, Gavin." He was so protective he made the President's bodyguards look like they were slacking off.

Gavin sighed. "Of course we would protect you. But we would also talk to you. This relationship needs communication to work, we need to talk to each other, share things. Talk to us, baby girl. We'd do the same for you."

Her anger melted and she leaned back against Trace. "You're right. I should have talked to you. It just caught me by surprise. I love you guys so much. I don't think I could stand losing you."

Colin held open his arms. "Come here and give me a cuddle."

With a smile, she walked over to him, letting him draw her down to lie next to him on the sofa.

"I'm sorry," she said.

He patted her bottom. "You should have told us. Do you really think we care about some rumors? Did you think we'd think less of you?"

Dropping her head, she nodded. "I was an idiot. I know you would never think less of me because of her, I was just taken by surprise and I never want anything to hurt you guys, especially me."

"Do you know what *does* hurt us?" Gavin asked.

"What?"

"Knowing that you don't trust us."

Her jaw dropped. "What are you talking about?"

"I had hoped that you would trust us a little by now, at least enough to let us help you, to know we wouldn't leave you. You would have gone off to meet that bitch alone and given her a huge chunk of your inheritance. Do you know how dangerous that is? She could have done anything to you and we would have had no idea."

Lila sat up and stared at them. "I do trust you. I know it may not seem like it, but I just wanted to protect you guys."

"Not your job, honey," Gavin replied. "Our job is to take care of you. Yours is to let us. And to love us."

"I do. I do."

Lila stood and walked slowly over to Gavin who was now sitting on an armchair. She owed it to them to completely open up to them. Kneeling in front of him, she took his hands in hers.

"I've always found it hard to trust. When I was young, my mother would always promise that things would get better. Then she'd start drinking and doing drugs and the men would be back with their mean eyes and their grabby hands. I remember the first time one hit me; I must have been around six. My mother just sat there and laughed. I couldn't see out of that eye for nearly a week. That's when I started hiding in the alley when men came over."

"Baby," Gavin began, reaching for her, his eyes softening.

Lila shook her head. "No, let me finish before I lose my nerve. I don't like to talk about my life before Clay found me in that alley, because I had no life. More than likely I would have ended up like my mother, whoring for enough money to buy booze and drugs. The thought of it frightens me. But I didn't end up like that because of Clay and you guys. I owe him, all of you, everything. Clay gave me a life, showed me love and gave me you three. The thought of that woman touching any of you with her filth, I just, I would do anything to protect you guys."

Gavin sighed and clasped her face in his hands. "And we feel the same way about you. We want to protect you, and you're making it very hard."

"I'm sorry, I do trust you, I do. I knew you wouldn't blame me for her actions, but I guess I've always had problems believing that I deserved to be here, believing that I deserved your love. Just give me some more time, love me, and don't ever leave me."

Gavin drew her up, holding her close. "We're here for you, baby girl. Always."

"Umm, what are we going to do about her?"

"Oh, we're going to make sure that she never bothers you again," Trace said with some relish. "And we're going to make it very clear that if she tries to spread one nasty rumor that her life won't be worth living.

"What are you planning? Are you going to meet with her?"

"Yep," Gavin answered.

"I'm coming too, then," she insisted.

"Like hell," Gavin said with a frown. "I don't want you anywhere near her. You're going to stay right here."

"No way, I'm coming too. Remember how you said we needed to talk things through? This can't be all one way. I get that you want to protect me, but she's my mother and while I'm glad you guys are helping me, I have to see this through."

All three men looked at each other. Trace nodded. Good, one down. Colin shrugged. Number two was on her side. Now for the hardest one. She looked up at Gavin. He was scowling, obviously wishing he could keep her here. But he couldn't wrap her up in cotton wool. She loved the way they looked after her, but she wouldn't be smothered.

"We'd be there with her," Trace told him. "And it would show that bitch that we are all on the same page. Plus give Lila some closure."

Lila bit her tongue, just waiting.

"All right," Gavin gave in. "But you, baby girl, will do exactly as you are told."

She nodded. "I will. I promise."

"Now, we get to address the fact you kept something big from us," Gavin said darkly. He set her off his lap then left the room.

"Where is he going?"

"To get some supplies," Colin told her, smiling wickedly. "Strip."

"What?"

"Strip off. Slowly. We want to watch."

Trace nodded, his eyes darkening.

She blushed. "I can't just strip."

"Sure you can. Unless you want one of us to do it. But my hand is itching to spank that ass, so I'm thinking you don't," Colin told her.

She started to strip. By the time Gavin returned, she was completely naked. He held something long and rounded in his hand as well as a tube of lube.

"W-what's that?" she asked, gulping.

"This is a butt plug." It was slim at the tip and thick at the base where it flared out. She gulped. Yeah, no way was that thing going up her ass.

"I didn't know you were into butt plugs," she tried to joke. "Need a bit of help with that?"

Gavin grinned evilly. "Oh, that isn't for me and I have all the help I need."

Colin patted his lap. "Come here, shorty and lay over my lap."

Lila shook her head. "I don't want to."

Colin looked at her steadily. "Procrastinating isn't going to help, Lila. Come here now."

"But Gavin's going to stick that up my ass!" she wailed.

Colin's lips twitched. "That he is, and I'm going to help him. Having to wear this all night will remind you how much we love you and want to take care of you. It will also help prepare you to take all three of us." He tapped his thigh. "Come here now."

Lila's legs moved even as her mind screamed at her to turn and run away. But why would she run? This is where she wanted to be, with these three men.

She let Colin help her lie over his lap, her body rested on the sofa, her bottom facing Gavin.

"Okay, little one," Colin said. "I want you to relax for us. The more you relax the easier this will be."

"Easy for you to say," she snapped back. "You're not the one about to get a plug up your ass."

Slap!

"Hush," Gavin told her strictly. "Relax."

What the hell did he expect from her? He couldn't order her to relax and expect her to instantly obey him.

Colin's hands rubbed over her back, massaging and she gradually found herself doing just that. Then his hands moved to her bottom, parting her cheeks. She whimpered as something cold was dabbed on her asshole.

Oh hell, this was so embarrassing.

"I can't believe you're doing this to me," she groaned as Gavin slipped a single finger deep inside her asshole.

"Shh, baby, there's nothing to be embarrassed about," Colin attempted to soothe her.

"Gavin has a finger up my ass!" she screeched.

"Well, I'm about to have two," Gavin replied matter-of-factly, before pushing another finger inside her tight hole.

She moaned, utterly humiliated and yet incredibly turned on. Moisture coated her folds as Gavin thrust his fingers across nerve endings she never knew existed.

"God, that is so hot," Trace told her. "I can't wait to have that ass. We'll have to take care to prepare you, though. This won't be the last butt plug you have up your ass and each one will be bigger than the last."

"Get ready, Lila," Colin told her. "Take a deep breath in. There you are. Now breathe out."

As she exhaled, Gavin slid the butt plug deep inside her. She felt full to bursting as she gasped for breath. Colin spread her legs, his fingers dipping down to brush between her silken folds. Colin rubbed his finger over her clit, swirling around it, tapping it.

"Oh, oh, please," she cried out, writhing.

Sharp slaps landed on her ass. They shocked her, adding to her pleasure. Oh, Christ, she couldn't stand this.

"Please what?" Colin asked.

"Please let me come, I need to," she begged.

"Hmm, I don't think so," Gavin said evilly. "Good girls get to come. Not bad ones who keep things from their men."

No. No, they wouldn't.

"Maybe after you've held this plug in your ass for a few hours, we might take pity on you," Trace added, giving her ass another slap. She cried out as she felt that smack in her clit. Oh hell, it wouldn't take much to send her over. Just a bit more.

But then Colin took his finger from her clit.

"No!"

Someone lifted her up. Gavin. He leaned in and kissed her. Then he pulled back, grinning down at her. "Yes, I think this is exactly what she needs to remind her that we take her safety very seriously."

LILA WAS SO FUCKING HORNY, she was about to explode. She couldn't believe they just expected her to sit here and watch TV with a damn plug up her ass!

She shifted around on the sofa, sandwiched between Trace and Gavin. Colin sat at her feet, between her legs, meaning she couldn't even rub her thighs together for some relief. As hot and hard as her clit felt it might just be enough to get her off too.

Gavin laid his hot hand on her thigh. "Stay still."

There was something incredibly arousing about being naked while the three of them were dressed. Decadent. Naughty.

"I can't." She whimpered.

Colin turned, now kneeling between her legs, his attention on her pussy. "She's dripping with arousal."

"Oh God." She closed her eyes, so embarrassed.

Trace clasped the back of her neck, squeezing lightly. "Open your eyes."

She forced her eyes open, looking up into his gaze. He studied her. "Look down at Colin and ask him to pretty please eat your pussy."

Oh no. No way. She gaped at Trace. His lips twitched once, but he didn't smile.

"You're not serious."

"Oh, I am. Ask him nicely."

Fuck.

She turned to look down at Colin. She needed to come so badly she knew she was going to do it. She just had to get it over with.

"Colin, p-please eat my pussy."

Colin smiled. "I thought you'd never ask."

As though she'd been the one holding back. He grasped hold of her hips, dragging her forward and spreading her wide. Trace and Gavin each grabbed a leg, pulling it over their laps and holding her open. Colin licked at her clit, lightly at first his movement growing firmer, faster.

"Oh. Oh."

"I think our girl likes having her butt plugged," Gavin mused as he pinched her nipple.

She pushed her chest out, the sharp pain only adding to her pleasure.

"I can't wait to take her there," Trace answered, circling her other nipple with his finger. "I wish she was ready. I think we should plug her every night."

No, she wouldn't be able to stand it. Her head thrashed back and forth until Gavin grasped hold of her chin, turning her face towards his.

"Come for us, baby." He dropped his mouth to hers, taking her lips with his, commanding her, devouring her. His mouth muffled her scream as she came, her body shaking so hard she was worried for a moment that she'd shake her way right off the sofa. But they held her steady, like she knew they would.

But before she could start to drift down, they moved her, placing her on her knees in front of the sofa. She turned, watching as the three of them stripped. She barely held back a whimper of need.

"You're all so beautiful."

Colin grinned, but Gavin just shook his head. "Men aren't beautiful."

They were. And she couldn't believe they were all hers. Gavin sat on the sofa, his cock hard and thick. He drew her between his open legs. "Suck me down."

Yes. God, yes.

She licked her way around the head as she felt hands on her hips, drawing her back. She paused for a moment, looking behind her to find Trace kneeling there. He grinned at her before plunging deep.

"Oh hell!" She felt impossibly full, the plug in her ass making her so tight.

"Damn it, Trace, easy with her," Colin said.

"She needed it, didn't you, Lila?" Trace asked.

"Yes," she managed to get out. "Move, please move."

Pleasure swamped her and she knew it wouldn't take much until she came again. Gavin turned her attention back to his cock, and she opened her mouth as he guided his firm shaft into her mouth. She sucked on him, loving the taste of him, wanting to make him fly like she just had.

Trace thrust back and forth, his movements growing harder, faster. He reached around to flick her clit and she cried out around Gavin's cock.

"Jesus, Trace. I'm gonna come if you keep that up," Gavin moaned.

Wasn't coming the point. She slowly took Gavin's cock into her mouth then sucked hard as she moved back up.

"Oh hell. I'm gonna come. Fuck!" Gavin yelled out as he came. She swallowed him down, licking at him, getting every drop. As she drew back, Colin shoved Gavin aside, looking down at her intently.

"My turn."

Oh yeah.

She licked at him, suckled on him, took just the head of him into her mouth, swirling her tongue around him.

"Enough playing, Lila," Trace told her. "I'm close. So close. Time to come again."

She whimpered.

"Take Colin deep, little girl," Gavin whispered from beside her as he reached down and replaced Trace's finger on her clit. Trace grabbed hold of her hips and thrust deep. Hard.

Oh hell.

She screamed as she came. Then Trace gave two final thrusts, following her over.

"Fuck. Fuck." Colin grasped hold of her head and drove in deep.

She swallowed him down.

Okay, so maybe being made to wait wasn't a terrible thing. Not that she'd tell them that.

11

Lila took a deep breath as they pulled up outside the old church. She was in the passenger seat while Gavin drove. Trace and Colin had driven in earlier, but had parked well back and continued in on foot to scout the place out first, wanting to make sure there were no surprises.

Gavin parked and climbed out, staring around him. She waited until he came around and opened her door, taking his hand as he helped her down. He kept hold of her hand as they walked towards the church. The door opened as they approached and her mother stepped out, her face screwed up in a scowl.

"What the fuck is he doing here?" she snarled, glaring at them both.

Gavin kept her close. He'd drilled the rules into her on the way over. She wasn't to approach her mother. Under no circumstances was she to get between him and her mother. She was to obey him immediately, no matter what he ordered her to do.

On the drive over, Trace had called to tell them he'd spotted a man with her mother. That shouldn't have surprised her. She wondered whose idea this had been, her mother's or this myste-rious man's?

"Gavin is here to support me," Lila told her.

Her mother's gaze left her face to look behind her.

"We came to tell you that I'm not paying you."

"You sure about that?" A deep voice asked from behind her mother and an older, large man stepped out. He might have been handsome and fit in his day, but his muscles had turned to fat and his hair was thin and graying. His small, beady eyes were hard and mean. "No money means the gloves are off, sweetheart," he said with a sneer. She shivered, not liking the cold way he stared at her. "Are you sure your boyfriend here wants his reputation dragged through the mud?"

Lila squeezed Gavin's hand to keep him quiet. "I'm not afraid of you, and I won't be blackmailed. Those who knew Clay, who know us, they know the truth and their opinions are the only ones that count. You can't hurt us. And I won't let you have one cent of Clay's money. Go back to the hole you crawled out of," she directed at her mother. "And don't ever come back. As far as I'm concerned I have no mother."

"You little bitch," Abigail snarled, her hands curling into fists. "After all I did for you. You're nothing but a money hungry cunt. I wish to God I had gotten rid of you. If I'd had the money I would have. You've been nothing but a fucking burden around my neck since you were born. Only reason I kept you around was because I thought you might make me some cash. I was planning on selling you to men who like 'em young. Think you're so great now, don't you? But you're nothing but a whore's daughter. This lot will move on once they get enough of your cunt."

"Enough," Gavin roared, taking a step forward, his hands clenched into fists.

"No, Gavin," Lila said urgently, reaching out to grab hold of his arm with both hands. "She's not worth it. She's not worth anything. The only good thing you ever did was give me up and I'm sure you got your money's worth for that, didn't you?".

She knew from the look on her mother's face that she was right. She'd often wondered if Clay had paid her mother off and now she knew. Nausea filled her at how close she'd come to being stuck with this woman. How long would it have been until Abigail had sold her to some sick asshole?

"Go home and don't come back," Lila told her with disgust.

"I don't think so." The big man stepped towards them and suddenly Colin and Trace stepped out from the trees, moving towards them steadily, flanking Lila and Gavin.

"Oh, I think so, buddy," Trace snarled. "Stand back."

"Lila, get in the truck," Gavin told her.

She turned immediately and walked away, ignoring Abigail's calls. Sitting in the truck, she waited for her men, her stomach bubbling with the need to throw up. Sweat ran down her back, her hands shaking as adrenaline flowed through her.

Trace turned back to look at her worriedly. He sent her a smile even as Gavin stiffened and Colin braced himself as though expecting someone to attack. She couldn't hear what they were saying but their body language spoke volumes. Her men were furious and Abigail—Lila shivered as she made eye contact—was absolutely livid.

Suddenly the man with Abigail let out a loud roar and stepped forward, his meaty fist raised. Lila watched, breathless, as Gavin easily blocked his punch with his arm, before quickly following up with a jab to the large man's gut then a quick uppercut.

The older man fell back, holding his hand up to his nose. Her mother stepped forward, fluttering around him as he waved her off with a snarl. Gavin said something more before he, Trace and Colin turned and came back towards her.

Gavin hopped into the driver's seat as Colin and Trace climbed in the back.

"What did you say to him?" she asked as Gavin spun the truck around and took off. His knuckles were white where he clasped the steering wheel tightly. "Do you think they'll leave?"

"Oh, they'll leave," Colin answered her. "Jake will make sure of that even if we didn't. Before we came, I called the Banning brothers and told them that they had a couple of trespassers hanging out on their land. They'll be here with Jake shortly to escort your mother and her companion out of town. Nobody is happy with the threats they made. We look after our own in Haven."

Gavin reached over and grabbed her hand, squeezing tight. "Don't worry, baby girl, you won't ever see them again. I promise."

Relief made her light-headed and she closed her eyes.

"We told them that they would never get a cent out of us, no matter what they did," Gavin told her. "I also made it abundantly clear that should they ever approach you, call you, write to you then I had a number of ways of getting rid of bodies."

"They believed you?" she asked incredulously.

Gavin stopped beside Trace's truck and turned to look at her, his eyes cold and deadly. "Baby girl, I meant every word. No one threatens the people I love."

"They knew it too," Colin added as he undid his seatbelt. "They won't be bothering you again."

"But if they ever do then you tell us straight away," Gavin added, his face so intense that she couldn't deny him even if she had wanted to.

"I promise."

Colin and Trace climbed out and got into Trace's truck.

"Okay, baby girl," Gavin said, running his thumb over her knuckles. "Let's go home."

12

She needed to stop thinking. It was driving her insane. Over and over in her head, Lila heard her greedy, self-involved mother telling her how much she ever regretted having her.

Lila rubbed her head, trying to get that woman's voice out of her head, but nothing helped. Nothing except keeping busy. She stared around the house, but there was nothing left to do. She'd done all the cleaning, washing and ironing. She'd even ironed everyone's underwear for goodness sake.

She needed to get out of the house, surely that would help. Get some exercise. She put on some long, tight pants and a T-shirt before heading out of the house. Entering the cool, dark stables, she looked around for Ron. Shrugging when she couldn't see him, she saddled Sunshine herself, placing her cell phone in the saddlebags.

"This is what I needed, isn't it boy?" she said, patting Sunshine five minutes later as they moved towards the hilly area of the ranch. The peace of the day soothed her. What did she care what that old bitch said? She wasn't her family. She may have given birth to her but Clay had raised her.

Directing Sunshine towards the track that led to lookout point, Lila tried to clear her head, to just live in the moment. This area of the ranch was beautiful, not suitable for ranching, but for biking or riding it was ideal. Reaching the summit, she climbed off Sunshine and took in a few deep gulps of air.

Acres of land lay out before her. Below lay the deep lake. Maybe she could convince the guys to take a day off and they could all spend the day there, she'd pack a picnic, bring a blanket and maybe forget about that horrible encounter with her mother.

"I hate you," she cried out, surprising herself. "How dare you treat me like dirt? What kind of mother gives up her child? How could you? You didn't deserve me!"

As she finished, her chest heaving, she felt lighter, more at peace. This is what she'd needed, to get all the anger out. She sat, breathing deeply for a long moment before standing.

"I have no mother," she said without any anger. "And that's okay with me."

She turned to Sunshine. "Come on, fella. Let's go back to my men."

A yipping noise made her pause and listen. She shook it off as her imagination. Then it came again. Leaving Sunshine tethered to a branch, she moved towards the sound. Suddenly, down the ravine she caught a flash of movement.

"A dog," she said with amazement. "How the hell did he get down there?"

The dog, as if hearing her, yipped again but barely moved.

"Shit. He must be stuck," she muttered to herself. "Don't worry, boy, I'm coming." With no thought to her own safety, she started down the incline.

"HEY, BRO, HOW WAS YOUR DAY?" Colin called out cheerfully to Gavin as he climbed from his truck.

Gavin shrugged, looking tired. "Okay, I guess."

"You seen Lila today?" Colin asked as he stepped up beside him to walk inside.

Gavin's face instantly dimmed, worry taking over. Colin knew how he felt. Since their confrontation with Lila's mother a few days ago, she'd withdrawn from them. He couldn't remember her smiling much since. She'd cleaned the house within an inch of its life, even going so far as to wash the first-story windows. Gavin had forbidden her from doing the second story as a cautionary measure.

Colin figured she would have gone on to clean them next if he hadn't. She seemed so driven, she couldn't sit still, couldn't relax, could barely sleep or eat.

He couldn't even come close to understanding how she was feeling. To have her own mother try to blackmail her then basically tell her she was never wanted. That had to be devastating, even though she hadn't seen her mother in years.

Colin couldn't imagine his own mother ever talking to him like that. The pain of losing his parents was still intense, even after all these years. But at least he'd experienced their love and affection and protection before losing them. Lila hadn't received any of those things from her mother.

"Nah, I just got in and she was asleep this morning when I left," Gavin replied. "She's so sad, it's killing me. Makes me wish I'd killed that bitch of a mother."

"I'll talk with her after my shower," he said.

Twenty minutes later, he raced through the house looking for her. It was his second attempt at searching her out. He'd tried her phone but it kept ringing then going to voicemail.

Trace walked through the front door, spotting him. "Sunshine is gone," Trace said. "No one saw her leave. Gavin is saddling our horses. We're going to head out to the lake."

LILA'S ENERGY WAS WANING. Fast. She stared down at the dog in her arms, grimacing at how bad he smelt. When she'd climbed down the hill, she'd discovered he was limping. After about twenty minutes of soft talking, she'd managed to get close to him. He'd sniffed her hand then gave her a lick. Poor thing was thin and dirty. Who knows where he'd come from or when his last meal had been.

By the time she'd managed to convince him to let her pick him up and managed to get back up to Sunshine, she'd been exhausted. She reached into the saddlebags to get her phone just as she heard it ring.

"Hello?"

"Lila! Where are you?" Colin's voice was sharp with worry.

She grimaced. "At my thinking spot. Doing a spot of dog rescue."

"What? Never mind, we'll be there soon."

He hung up and she stared down at the dog. "I think I'm in trouble, Sarge."

"Lila!"

She looked up at the yell, giving a sigh of relief as she saw Trace, Colin and Gavin riding towards her. They pulled up a few feet away and jumped down. The dog gave a warning growl.

"It's okay, they're with me."

"What the hell happened?" Gavin barked. "Why weren't you answering your phone?"

"I had to climb down a hill to get to this guy and then when I finally managed to carry him up, my phone was flat."

Colin moved forward, crooning to the dog in her arms. He reached out his hand and the dog gave it a suspicious lick. "Where did you come from?"

"I don't know but he's in pretty bad shape."

"You should have called us first," Gavin growled. "What if he'd attacked you?"

"He's got a sore paw, he can hardly move."

"Come here, boy." Colin pulled the dog from her arms, wrinkling his nose. "Someone needs a bath."

"We both do," she said wryly.

Gavin drew her close, hugging her. "I was out of my mind when I couldn't find you."

"I'm sorry," she told him.

By the time they reached the house Lila was so tired and in pain she felt nauseous. It had been a long trip, the men having to move slowly once darkness hit, climbing off their horses to walk while leading Sunshine. Sarge had limped along beside Lila, seemingly happy to follow them home.

Gavin reached up and pulled her off the horse, holding her close against his chest as he walked into the house. Trace led the horses away while Colin saw to the dog. Gavin walked into her bedroom and placed her on the bed.

Lila grabbed his hand as he went to remove her shoes. "Gavin, I'm okay," she told him. "I'm here and I'm all right."

His gaze snapped up to hers and she nearly flinched at the furious worry in his eyes. "What the hell were you doing? Why didn't you leave us a note?"

"I needed to get out of the house, to think. I'm sorry, I just didn't think about leaving a note. I had to get away."

"Not good enough. We could have been looking for you all night."

"Gavin, I'm okay," she told him again. "I'm here, safe with you."

Gavin shuddered, dropping his head. Then he stared straight at her.

"You terrify me," he told her. "You're so fragile and precious and you don't seem to know it! Don't you realize how much you mean to me? Since that encounter with your mother you've put up this barrier between us and I don't like it one bit. I get that you need to think things through and that your mother upset you, but you have to let us in."

"You're right. I did a lot of thinking. I've been letting Abigail get to me and that's exactly what she wanted. I'm not going to let her ruin my life. She didn't raise me or love me and she has no part to play in my life. You guys have always been there for me and I've been keeping a part of myself blocked off from you. It wasn't fair of me and I'm sorry."

Gavin leaned up and kissed her as he leaned back, she looked up and saw Colin and Trace standing there.

"You heard that?" she asked them. They nodded, smiling.

"How's Sarge?" she said to Colin.

"Sarge?" Trace asked.

"That's what I named him."

"He's fine. Undernourished, in need of a bath but I don't think his leg is broken but I'm going to take him into the clinic now." Colin kissed the top of her head and left.

"I'll grab a shower then cook some dinner," Trace told them.

She wrinkled her nose. "I need a shower too."

"I'll start a bath for you," Gavin told her. He picked her up, bringing her into the bathroom and setting her down on the sink as he started the bath. Then he gently stripped her, placing her into the water.

"You're so good to me."

"It's no less than you deserve, baby girl."

She lay silent for a long moment, just letting him take care of her. He swiped the cloth over her nipples, making her shiver with anticipation, then he moved down her stomach to between her legs, rubbing gently, his finger slipping between her legs to play with her.

"Gavin," she panted as arousal overtook her.

"Shh, just let me make you feel good." He circled her clit then flicked it. Back and forth. Round and round. Her whole body trembled. She needed the release, craved it. The only thing that would make it better was if he was inside her. It didn't take long until pleasure overtook her, tumbling through her until she let go in a huge rush.

"Ohh," she groaned as wave after wave continued to flood her with bliss. Gavin chuckled.

"Gav?" she asked a few minutes later, once her brain had started to function once more.

"Yeah, baby?" he asked.

"Can I ask you something?"

"Anything."

"Did you ever go searching for your parents?" she asked, opening her eyes to look at him.

He was staring off into the distance. "I already knew who my parents were, baby. When I was five my mother was killed. Drunk driver. My father lost it, went on a bender. Drinking, gambling, whoring, you name it, he did it."

Lila remained silent, watching him. He'd never told her about his parents before. She'd just assumed he knew little about them.

"When I was twelve, he got into a bar fight, hit a man too hard. The guy fell back and hit his head. Three days later they shut off the life support and my father ended up in jail for manslaughter and assault. That's the last I ever heard of him."

"Oh, Gavin." She clasped his hand in hers. "I'm so sorry."

He shrugged then ran his fingers down her cheek. "I guess it all worked out in the end, didn't it? I met Trace and Colin, then Clay adopted me and then he found you. And darling, there is nothing more important to me than you."

With a smile, she leaned up and kissed him.

13

L ila loaded the last of the shopping bags in the back of Clay's mammoth truck. It had been the only available vehicle left at the ranch this morning, so even though she wasn't that comfortable driving it she hadn't had much choice. They were low on groceries and she didn't want to have to ask the guys to take her every time she needed to go into town.

She'd driven into Freestown to do her shopping. The store in Haven was good for small things, but for a bigger shop she preferred Freestown. She heaved a bag of potatoes into the back. She really needed to get started on a vegetable garden.

To show her guys how much she appreciated them, she'd decided to do something special. She just needed to do a little bit of shopping first.

Crossing the road, she entered the lingerie store she'd spotted earlier. As soon as she saw the emerald green gown, she knew it was the one. It was sheer with just a bit of lace to cover her nipples and mound. Paying for the item, she walked out into the hot sunshine with a small smile on her face.

This was going to blow her men away. Opening the back door to the truck, she placed the bag on the seat.

"Like mother like daughter, huh?" a snide voice stated. Turning, Lila found a woman leaning against the back on the truck. She stepped back and closed the door. Why did this woman look familiar?

Sarge growled at the other woman surprising Lila because the friendly mutt seemed to like everyone.

"Excuse me?" Lila asked. What was she talking about?

"Born from a whore, become a whore," the girl sang.

Was she a few screws loose?

"You're not his girlfriend, you know. He's just using you. And no amount of lingerie or spa treatments is going to turn you into something you're not."

"Who are you talking about?" Lila asked.

"He might take you dancing, you might live in his home and answer his phone, but he's going to be *mine* forever."

Suddenly Lila remembered where she recognized her from. She was that waitress from Dirty Delights, the one who had spilled a drink on her.

"You were at Dirty Delights the other night. Who are you? Are you following me?" Lila asked, growing alarmed.

The other woman ignored her questions. "When I met your precious mommy a few weeks ago I couldn't believe my luck. At first, I couldn't understand what he saw in you, but after meeting your mother, I now understand. You're his whore. You're not his woman; you service the three of them. This is just a phase he needs to go through before he settles down with me. I understand. Then he'll come back to me, where he should be. You know, you should just cut your losses now, they'll never marry you. Do you even know your father? I suppose your mother could hardly narrow it down, could she?"

Lila was shocked, speechless. Her stomach had dropped at the mention of her mother. Which one of Lila's men was she talking about? She took a good look at the woman standing before her. She was dressed a lot nicer than the other night in black slacks and a white shirt. Was she even a waitress?

"How did you meet my mother?" Lila finally asked.

"She was asking questions about you. I was happy to answer. How do you think she knew you were at Dirty Delights that night?" the other woman scorned. "Because I called her of course."

"Who are you?" Lila asked again.

The other woman sneered. "None of your business, whore. I just came to deliver a message. Get your dirty whore hands off my man."

"Listen, I don't know who you are, or which one of my men you think is yours. But I am no whore. They are mine. So just stay away from me and them." Lila opened the driver's door and quickly jumped in, slamming and locking the door before she backed out of the park and drove off.

About twenty minutes out of town, her phone started ringing. Pulling safely over, she dragged it out of her bag, sighing with relief as she saw Trace's name.

"Hey, where are you?" Trace asked.

"About twenty minutes out of Freestown."

"Freestown?" Trace asked, sounding surprised. "What you doing there?"

"I got some groceries, we were nearly out," she explained. "I left a note." She was very careful to do that now.

"Oh, right, here it is. Sorry, I didn't see it. I was going to get groceries this afternoon. What vehicle are you driving?"

"Clay's truck."

"God damn it, that's too big for you to be driving around in. You better not be driving right now," he warned.

"No," she said with exasperation. "I pulled off the road, Trace. I'm not stupid."

"Well, good. I'll wait at the house for you to get here and help you unpack."

"I'm fine. You can go back to work."

"I'll see you soon," he said, ignoring her. "Drive slowly and carefully. If you run into any trouble I want you to call me. We really need to get you a car. See you soon."

"Love you."

"Love you too, sugar lips."

Rolling her eyes, a grin on her face, she drove home. Trace walked towards the truck as she pulled up. Opening her door, he caught her with a surprised chuckle as she launched herself at him.

"Now, that's a greeting a man could get used to," he told her, squeezing her tight. "You all right?" He stared at her in concern.

"Yep, fine."

"You didn't run into any trouble while driving the truck, did you?"

"No. I really am all right. I do have something to talk to you about, but it's nothing that can't wait until the ice cream is in the freezer. Should have just bought that in Haven."

He watched her for a long moment before nodding. "You go on inside. I'll haul these in and help you unpack."

Grabbing her handbag, she stuffed the bag with the sexy nightgown she'd bought into it and went inside to hide it in her room.

Fifteen minutes later everything was unpacked and she and Trace were sitting in the living room, each with a glass of iced tea.

"Right," he said, leaning forward with a look on his face which had her bottom clenching. "So are you going to tell me what you're fretting about or am I going to put you over my knee and start spanking until you start speaking?"

Her jaw dropped at his words. This wasn't Trace. Trace was the sane, calm one. That sounded more like something Gavin would say.

"You can't spank me to make me talk. That's mean!"

He snorted. Then his eyes turned devious. "Well maybe there is another way to get you to talk, how about erotic torture instead?" Reaching for her, he easily pulled her over his lap, holding her as she wriggled and swore.

God damn it, why couldn't she have fallen for a weakling? Someone she could have overpowered?

"Let me go, Trace!"

Trace chuckled. "I don't think so, I like you here like this, at my mercy, open to my touch." He raised her skirt and tugged down her panties.

"Trace!" she groaned.

"Part your legs, Lila."

She hesitated and he slapped her butt cheeks.

"Ow," she cried splitting her thighs apart. "You don't have to do this; I was going to tell you."

"I know, but this is more fun."

"Urgh, what's happened to you? Before you sounded just like Gavin and now you sound more like Colin."

Trace laughed and parted her bottom cheeks, running his finger up and down her crack before pushing it further down to her wet folds. He swirled his fingers in her juices, pushing two fingers deep inside her to thrust gently.

"Oh God," she cried out, arching back in reaction.

"Like that, baby?" he crooned.

"You know I do.".

"Good, then start talking." Damn it, she wasn't used to this dominant side of Trace.

"Trace! Couldn't we...you know? And then we'll chat?" He pulled his fingers from her pussy to tap her sensitive clit. She needed to come. Now!

"I don't think so," he said slowly, drawing his fingers back just as she'd been about to explode. "Talk to me then I'll let you come."

Lila groaned, unable to believe the depth of his cruelty. Part of her wished she'd just opted for the spanking.

Trace parted her bottom cheeks again, pressing one damp finger against her asshole. Lila clenched her teeth, her legs twitching as need flooded through her.

"Trace, no."

"Oh yes. Have I told you how much I love this ass? It's firm, round and so very sexy. I could stare at it for hours and not grow tired."

Her face was on fire even as her insides stirred, arousal building. Which was crazy, she shouldn't be turned on by this, should she?

A slap landed on her bottom, then Trace rubbed the slight sting, its heat spread from her ass throughout her body.

"Do you know a woman about half a head taller than me with long, dark brown hair and blue eyes?" she said quickly. "Slim build."

Trace pushed his finger further inside her asshole. "Possibly, sounds like a few women I know."

"I've never met her before, but she was waitressing at Dirty Delights the other night. She spilled a drink on me and I don't think it was accidental. Then today in Freestown she came up to me as I was about to drive home. She said she was the one who told my mother I was at Dirty Delights that night. She seems to think she has a claim on one of you and that when you grow tired of me you'll get rid of me for her because I'm a whore like my mother."

Trace swore and turned her over to hold her on his lap. "Baby, you know that's not true, don't you?"

"Course I do," Lila said indignantly. "I'm no whore and I know you guys love me, but this woman is obviously deranged and I'm worried about you guys. What if she tries to hurt one of you?"

"You're such a doll to worry about us, but you're the one she seems to be fixated on and I don't like it one bit. The only women we've had trouble with lately are your mother and Sara."

"Could it be Sara?" she asked. "She could have dyed her hair."

He looked thoughtful. "It's possible. But why would she be working as a waitress? I'll give Devon a call and get the names of all his waitresses."

Devon Fletcher owned Dirty Delights and had been a friend of Trace's for years.

Lila shook her head. "That's just it. I'm not sure she does work there. I didn't really think about it before, but don't all the waitresses wear little tank tops with the bar's logo on it?"

"Yeah, they do."

"This woman's top didn't have a logo. I think she was just pretending to be a waitress to get close to me."

"I don't like this one bit. From now on, you go nowhere alone, do you understand me? One of us will take you wherever you need to go."

"Trace," she began.

"No," he told her sternly. "This is not up for negotiation. You're under our protection. You break this rule, darling, and I will make any spanking you've received so far look like love taps."

Lila nodded.

"Answer me in words, Lila."

"Yes."

"Good girl," he murmured. "Don't worry, we'll take care of you."

"I know you will."

He grinned. "And right now I think you need some very special care, don't you?"

She answered his grin with one of her own, squealing as he

stood and swung her over his shoulder. With a slap to her butt, he raced up the stairs to her bedroom, where he took very, very good care of her.

Lila followed her men into the living room. Gavin and Colin sat on the sofa, while Trace took the armchair.

"What's wrong, baby?" Gavin asked in concern.

Trace answered him. "Lila has something to tell you both. Go ahead, honey."

She took a deep breath. "All right, just don't interrupt me until I'm done, okay?"

Colin and Gavin nodded. She paced, telling them about her encounter with the fake-waitress the other night and seeing her again this afternoon. Gavin went to interrupt a few times, but managed to stop himself.

"So," she finished. "Do either of you have any idea who this woman is?"

Gavin shook his head. "She could be any number of women from her description, except for the fact that she's crazy. You don't go anywhere by yourself from now on, understand me?"

Damn, she was going to be spending a lot of time at home. She wanted to argue but knew they were right, there was something wrong with this woman.

"Devon emailed me a list of waitresses at Dirty Delights," Trace said. "But we couldn't figure out who it might be. The only waitress with long, dark hair is Missy and she's not exactly slim."

Trace looked over at Colin. "There is one woman we thought it might be."

She stared at Colin, worried by how pale he was. "Are you okay? You're awfully quiet."

"Did she happen to have a necklace on? A locket with a gold chain?"

Lila screwed up her face in concentration. "Yeah. I think she might have. Why?"

He laughed derisively. "Because I gave her that locket."

"So you think it could be Sara?" Trace asked.

Colin nodded miserably, running his hand through his hair. "This is my fault. I brought this on us."

"No," she told him, moving over to sit on his lap. Colin pulled her close and rocked her. "None of this is your fault. Can you honestly tell me that you thought she would do this?"

"Hell no," he said emphatically. "She said I was disgusting. Why the hell would she think I was still interested in her after what she did?"

"She's obviously got problems," Gavin said in a low voice.

"None of this is your fault," Lila told him gently. "Was it my fault my mother came here, threatening us?"

"No," Colin said with a frown. "And I don't want you thinking that way."

"And I don't want you thinking this way."

Colin nodded and rocked back and forth, holding her tight.

"I think we need some extra security," Gavin said. He rose. "I'm going to go ring Matthias. He and his brothers can install an alarm."

"Do you think that's necessary?" Lila asked. "I mean, all she's really done is spill a drink on me. Well, and maybe she's been following me too."

The men looked at her.

"I just remembered what she said about Colin taking me dancing and my going to the spa. She must have been watching me."

Gavin stared at her. Hard. "She's obviously delusional if she thinks she and Colin have something going on. Who knows what she will do as time goes on and you're still here with us? I won't risk your safety, Lila."

Colin clasped her face in his hands. "Just let us take care of you, Lila. Please. I'd never forgive myself if she managed to hurt you."

Lila melted. "Okay, I promise. I'll do what you guys think is best."

14

Gavin stood, stretching with a yawn. "Time for bed." He held out a hand to Lila.

She shook her head. "I'm going to wait up for Colin."

Trace ran his hand over her head. "He could be gone all night, shorty."

Colin had been called out to a mare having trouble giving birth a few hours ago. Lila wanted a chance to talk to him alone, though, so she was prepared to wait.

Since her encounter with Sara a few days ago, Trace and Gavin had stuck close by. Sometimes she was lucky to use the bathroom alone. Colin, though, seemed to be avoiding her.

Yesterday, Matthias Simons had shown up with his two brothers, Beau and Jonty, and installed a state of the art security system. She hated to think of how much it had cost. Although she had a plan to pay them back.

"You need your rest, Lila," Gavin said worriedly, running the tips of his fingers over her cheek. "You're exhausted, baby girl."

"I know," she said. "But I'll sleep better if I can talk to Colin; he's getting even less sleep than I am."

Gavin and Trace looked at each other before Gavin sighed and leaned down to kiss her while Trace left the room.

"All right, but get some rest while you're down here, okay?" Gavin ordered gruffly. She saw the caring in his eyes and her body filled with warmth.

Trace returned with a pillow and a thick blanket which he tucked around her before placing a kiss on her forehead. "Night, baby."

"Night," she replied sleepily.

"Shit! Goddammit!"

Lila awoke with a gasp, sitting up as she heard a loud thud followed by more swearing.

"Hello?" she called out. "Colin?"

"Lila?" Light flooded the room and she groaned, placing her arm over her eyes.

"Shit, sorry baby, keep your eyes covered while I turn the lamp on instead."

When he sat beside her, she turned to him, lowering her arm slowly.

"What are you doing down here, Lila?" He cupped her face. "Are you feeling okay?"

Lila nodded. "I was waiting for you. I wanted to talk."

Colin frowned, tapping her nose in reproach. "You could have talked to me in the morning. You should be in bed, you won't get a good sleep down here and I could have been gone all night."

"I know, but it seems like I never get a moment alone with you now. Are you avoiding me?"

He was silent for a long moment then he sighed.

"Yeah, I have been."

She stared at him, aghast.

"Hey, Lila, no. Shit, I didn't mean it the way it sounded." He pulled her onto his lap and wrapping the blanket around her so she didn't get chilled.

"H-have you decided I'm more trouble than I'm worth?"

Colin glanced down at the precious bundle in his arms and cursed himself. They were always telling her how important communication was and here he was, shutting her out. And she'd assumed it was somehow her fault.

"Hey now, you get that thought out of your head right now. I am not avoiding you because of anything you've done or because I'm sick of you or any other nonsense like that. I was trying to keep my distance because," he sighed, "I was hoping to draw Sara out. I thought she might approach me if she saw I was alone. Although she's had plenty of chances to approach me in the last eight months so I'm not surprised that she's stayed hidden. I'm going to go to Hocken tomorrow, well, today actually." He glanced up at the clock which showed it was just after three in the morning.

"By yourself? No way," she said emphatically.

"Baby, I'm hoping that I can talk to her, convince her that there is nothing between me and her."

"And what if she won't listen?" Lila demanded. "What if she pulls a gun on you?"

Colin smiled slightly. "I hardly think she's going to do that."

"You don't know that. You guys think she's dangerous enough to watch me like a hawk, to install an expensive alarm system and yet you're just going to go and confront her alone? I don't think so."

Colin stared down at her, wondering how he'd gotten so lucky.

He brushed her silky hair back off her face. "How the hell did I get someone as wonderful as you?"

Lila blushed, smiling shyly. "Just lucky, I guess."

He grinned.

"You know, some of us are trying to sleep," Gavin growled from the doorway. His voice sounded grumpy but there was a smile on his face.

"Sorry," Lila said quickly, trying to rise. Colin held her firmly then stood, keeping her tucked in against his chest.

"We were just on our way up."

"Colin's planning on going to Hocken to confront Sara," Lila tattled on him. "Alone."

Gavin immediately scowled. "Like hell."

Colin sighed. Sometimes Gavin seemed to forget he was a grown man.

"Gavin—" he began.

"We'll all go," Gavin said emphatically.

"We can't all go," Colin tried to explain patiently as he climbed the stairs, Lila still held protectively in his arms.

"You're right," Gavin agreed, surprising him. "Lila and Trace can stay here. You and I will go."

"Hey," Lila protested as Colin carried her into her room and placed her on the bed.

"What's going on?" Trace said tiredly as he stumbled into the room, heading straight towards the bed. He instantly snuggled next to Lila, his nose nudging her breast. Lucky bastard. Colin's cock twitched, rising. *Down boy.*

He heard Gavin explaining his plan for tomorrow as he moved into the bathroom. When he re-entered the room, everyone was in bed.

Gavin frowned. "Trace is busy tomorrow, he can't watch over Lila."

"I've got two new horses arriving," Trace added.

"I don't need someone to watch over me," Lila grumbled.

"It's okay," Colin said. "I'll go by myself."

Gavin and Lila shook their heads. "Lila and I will go with you," Gavin said. "She's safer with us."

Colin shook his head but he was too tired to argue any further. "Fine," he said. "Now can we get some sleep?"

15

Colin squeezed Lila's hand as he walked down the main street of Hocken. He didn't know what he'd been expecting, to have everyone stare at him? Yell at him? Run him out of town?

Instead no one gave him a second look. They didn't recognize him. It was actually kind of disappointing. He'd spent so long thinking over what had happened, being haunted by it, and to realize that they had forgotten him as soon as he left town...

He shook his head, trying to gather his thoughts as they approached the vet surgery.

"You should stay out here with Gavin," he said to Lila, not liking that she was here one bit.

Lila shook her head and Gavin just stared at him. Neither of them, it seemed, was prepared to let him do this alone.

When they walked inside there was a young woman he didn't recognize behind the front desk.

"Hello," she said with a bright smile. "How can I help?"

"I'm looking for Sara Monroe," he said.

Immediately the smile dimmed and a wary look came into her eyes. "She doesn't work here anymore."

A mix of relief and disappointment surged through him.

"Jess?" A large man stepped into the office from the back. "Is my next appointment here yet?"

"Hi Zach," Colin said quietly, wondering if his friend would look at him with disgust or pity. Lila pressed tighter against his side. Gavin slung his arm around Lila's shoulders and patted him on the back.

"Colin!" Zach said with surprise and a smile of greeting crossed his face. "It's been a long time since I saw your ugly mug. What are you doing here? You looking for a job?"

Colin was shocked by the friendly response. He'd hoped for politeness at the most. "Ahh, no, I came here to see Sara actually."

Zach scowled. "Why would you want to talk to her? Wait a minute," he added before Colin could reply. "We'll be in my office, Jess, can you let me know when my next appointment arrives?"

Jess nodded, looking at them curiously.

"Come on through," Zach directed.

Colin led the way, still holding Lila's hand.

"Have a seat," Zach said, sitting behind his large desk. Colin seated Lila then took one himself. Gavin stood at the back of the room, his back against the wall, arms crossed over his chest. He glared at Zach, obviously trying to intimidate him.

Zach just grinned.

"This is my brother, Gavin," Colin introduced. "And our girl-friend, Lila."

Lila sent him a surprised smile, then reached out and grabbed his hand again. No way was he hiding their relationship. If people in this town didn't like it, well, he really didn't care.

Zach's smile grew wider. "Pleased to meet you both. So tell me, why are you here looking for Sara?"

Colin explained what had happened. Zach's smile faded and his face grew concerned. "Why the hell did you bring Lila here then? I had to let her go after you left. She started acting really weird, flying off the handle at nothing then all weepy the next minute. She was making a lot of mistakes too. I can't believe all the trouble she's causing. I hope you don't believe that we wanted you to leave, Colin. You didn't really give us a chance to talk to you before you left, but Alex and I wanted you to stay. We always knew Sara was a bit unstable, but we never thought she'd react the way she did."

Zach leaned back, running his hand over his face. "Unfortunately, she had a number of friends who loved drama. It would have died down eventually, once people realized what was going on. But you know small towns, they thrive on gossip. We wanted you to stay, Colin, but we also understood why you had to go. Seems like it worked out best for you anyway."

Zach winked at Lila. Colin felt gut-punched. He thought everyone had turned away from him, including Zach and Alex.

"I thought you were disgusted by my lifestyle."

"Well, now, that would be a bit hypocritical of me, wouldn't it?" Zach replied with a sly grin.

Hell, Colin should have guessed that Zach and his partner, Alex, liked to share women.

"Unfortunately for you, Sara became fixated on you, seems she still is. I don't know where she is, either. She left town a few months ago. If you find her, I'd sure like to know."

Colin nodded and stood, reaching out to shake Zach's hand.

"Next time you're in town, come have a beer with me and Alex, hear?" Zach offered as he walked them out.

"Sure," Colin said, although he had no real intention to ever come back. This place held too many bad memories.

"Nice to meet you all. Ahh, here is my appointment. Come in, Mrs. Flanders. How is Fluffy today?"

Colin walked out in a slight state of shock, letting Lila and Gavin lead him to Gavin's truck and drive him home.

LILA WAS GOING INSANE. Two weeks had passed with no sign of Sara and she was ready to explode. She was so bored she was scrubbing toilets. She was fed up with being confined to the house; she couldn't even ride Sunshine without an escort. It sucked, big time.

The phone rang and she raced for it, picking it up.

"Hello," she said breathlessly.

"Hey, girlfriend," Laken replied, sounding much happier than she had in a long time. "Guess what?"

"What?" Lila asked, sitting on the sofa.

"I'm opening a shop!" Laken squealed.

"What? You're doing what?"

"I'm opening a clothing store. I have heaps of clothes I've made over the last few years that have never been worn and I've been working on some new pieces since I got back. I also have a couple of friends who are making clothing and want somewhere to sell them. So I thought, why not open a store? I can't live off my dads forever."

"Laken! That's so exciting!" Lila said, happy for her. They spoke for a few moments about the details.

"Anyway, that's not the only reason I'm calling," Laken told her. "I have a favor to ask."

"Sure, shoot." Lila was happy to do whatever she could to help her friend.

"I know you can't do anything until this bitch is found, but I wondered if you'd work for me once everything calms down. I'm not sure how much I can pay you, but I need time to make the clothes so I'm going to need help in the shop. Luckily, it comes with a small apartment over it and the landlord gave me a good deal."

"Of course I will," Lila told her. "I'd love to."

"Yay! James and Rye are fixing it up this week, and then I'll just need to spend the following week getting everything set up and doing some marketing, which isn't my strong point."

"Man, I wish I could help you with all that." It was starting to feel like she was being punished for what Sara had done.

"I know. You know, the doors would be locked and it would be just me there. Well, and Savannah said she'd help too. Actually, I think I'll ask her to help with the marketing, isn't that what she used to do?"

"Yeah, I'm sure she'd be happy to help. And I don't see how I'm any safer here than I would be at your shop, as long as the doors remained locked."

"I'd love to have your help, but only if you're sure it's safe."

Lila bit her lip. "Let me see what I can do."

It had taken a lot of begging, yelling before her men agreed to let her go help Laken set up her shop. Of course there were a number of rules she had to promise to follow first before they would even let her out of the house.

But she'd follow whatever rules they wanted as long as she got to leave the house. She bounced up and down in excitement as Trace drove her into town.

"Poor baby, it's been so hard on you, being on lockdown, hasn't it?" he said sympathetically.

Lila nodded. "A whole month and nothing, I really think she's given up."

"I hope so," he said as he pulled up outside the shop Laken had rented. Coming around, he opened her door and helped her down. "But that doesn't mean you can relax your guard. Remember the rules."

"I know, no going anywhere. Doors must remain locked. I have to stay with Laken or Savi at all times and you will pick me up at four."

"Good girl." Leaning down, he gave her a kiss then knocked on the front door. Laken opened it with a squeal and threw her arms around Lila.

"Make sure this door remains locked," Trace told them all sternly. All three girls nodded solemnly and locked the door behind him, giggling as they got to work.

They worked hard all day, cleaning the place and unpacking boxes. At three o'clock they sat back and looked at what they had achieved.

"Thanks so much you guys," Laken said. "I couldn't have done all this without you."

Lila and Savi smiled and squeezed her hands.

"I'll get to work on the website tomorrow," Savi promised. "I've got flyers ready to go, but we'll need signage too."

"And I'll be back tomorrow to help you do a display," Lila said.

"You're the best friends I could ask for. But since this is our first day I think we deserve a little celebration, what do you think? I have some bubbly upstairs, let me go get it and we'll have a congratulatory drink." Laken stood and ran off.

Savi groaned. "I don't know where she finds her energy. I can hardly keep my eyes open. Ahh, crap," she said, trying to rise off the chair she was sitting in. "I forgot the flyers I'm meant to deliver tomorrow, they're out the back."

Lila shook her head. "Stay there, you're tuckered out. I'll get them."

Savi sat back with a sigh, closing her eyes. "Thanks. They're in a white box by the door."

Humming to herself, Lila walked into the back, frowning at the thin stream of sunshine coming in the open back door. Laken must have forgotten to shut it when she went upstairs. Walking towards it, she froze in shock as someone moved to her right.

"Sara," she said, standing very still as the other woman walked towards her, an evil smile on her lips and a small handgun in her hand. "What are you doing here?"

"I think that's fairly obvious. You wouldn't listen to my warning, so I'm here to take care of you and get my man out of your clutches."

"Colin is not your man. And he never will be." Lila needed to get Sara out of here before Savi and Laken got involved.

"What the hell is going on?" Laken asked as she stepped through the doorway, holding a bottle of wine and some glasses.

Sara turned towards Laken, momentarily distracted.

"Laken, down!" Lila screamed as she dived for Sara. The gun flew from Sara's hand as both women landed heavily on the concrete floor. Lila lay there, trying to catch her breath. Sara let out a scream of fury and, rolling, threw herself on top of Lila. She was larger and stronger, but Lila wasn't daunted.

Sara went straight for her hair, pulling it strongly before landing a punch to Lila's face. Lila gasped in pain, trying to fight her way free, clawing, scratching, kicking.

Suddenly Sara was shoved away from her and Lila looked up to see Laken standing over the other woman, her chest heaving.

Sara scuttled back a few inches, panting heavily, her hair scruffy and her clothes in a mess. A thin trail of blood ran down one cheek. She attempted to rise to her feet.

"Oh, I'd stay right there if I were you," Savi said fiercely. Lila glanced over to find Savannah holding the gun, aiming it right at Sara.

Lying back, Lila gave a sigh of relief, trying desperately to catch her breath, her whole body aching. Holy hell, she'd be lucky if her men ever let her out of their sight after this.

"Oh God, I'll call for help," Laken said, turning and moving up the stairs once more.

"You bitches!" Sara screeched.

"Shut up," Savannah said fiercely.

Lila just stared at Sara.

"He was meant to be mine. Mine."

"No, he was always mine," she told the other woman as she heard sirens. She started to breathe more easily as Jake entered followed by Duncan. Her men would be here soon. Then she'd know she was safe.

Lila lay in bed that night, completely surrounded by warm, protective bodies. Her men had pulled up outside Laken's store just as Jake had been taking Sara away in cuffs, the crazy woman screaming expletives, all aimed at Lila.

After the paramedics had checked Lila over and given her the all clear, they'd gathered her up, holding her close. Much as Max and Logan were doing with Savannah.

Duncan Jones had even shown up, dragging Laken into his arms, despite her protests. Poor Laken, she was furious at herself for leaving the back door unlocked while she went upstairs. She'd only intended to get the wine and come straight back but her phone had rung while she was upstairs and she'd gotten caught up, allowing Sara, who must have been watching, to sneak in.

After she'd answered a few questions for Jake, her men had taken her home, treating her like fragile glass the entire time. And she had to admit that she'd felt kind of fragile. She had a swollen eye and bruises over most of her body.

"I can't believe she tried to kill me," Lila said, still in shock.

"Shh." Gavin kissed her gently. He ran his hand down her

body. They hadn't stopped touching her since they'd gotten home. "It's over now, you're safe."

"I'm so glad you're safe," Colin told her from her other side. Trace lay across her legs.

"I don't think I can sleep," she confessed. "Every time I close my eyes I know I'm going to see her standing there with that gun." She let out a sob.

"If she visits you in your dreams then we'll be here, chasing her away," Gavin murmured.

They held her as she cried, loved her when she begged them to, held her as she slept and shook her awake when she cried out.

They were everything she could ever want and more.

EPILOGUE

"Lila Stacia Richards," Gavin boomed, his voice shaking the house.

Lila jumped up as Trace and Colin turned to look at her in interest. Colin leaned forward and switched off the movie they'd been watching. Gavin had gone to the study to do some work earlier, leaving them to lounge on the sofa.

"Uh-oh," she said. It had been three weeks since Sara had tried to kill her and Lila was finally starting to sleep without nightmares. But it was a slow process. And she knew Laken and Savannah still had nightmares as well.

Lila stared around, looking for a place to hide, futile as she knew that move would be.

"Lila," Gavin growled, walking into the room, his face thunderous.

"What did you do?" Colin asked with some amusement. He'd had his own nightmares about what had happened, and she'd often had to wake him up, hold him tight until he could sleep again.

"Umm." She hesitated, looking at Gavin. "I was just trying to do something nice," she said desperately, guessing what the issue was.

Gavin placed his hands on his hips. "What have we told you about your money?"

"I didn't try to give it to you." She stepped back, covering her backside with her hands.

"No, but what did you do?"

She bit her lip. "I paid some bills."

"You more than paid some bills, Lila. You paid every bill," he roared. "Come here." He crooked his finger at her.

Stepping over, she expected him to immediately pull her over his lap and start spanking her. Instead, Gavin surprised her by tipping her face up and kissing her gently on the lips. "I appreciate the thought, baby girl. I know you just want to help out. But you know we didn't want you trying to pay us back and we told you what would happen if you did, didn't we?"

"Well, technically you said you'd spank me if I tried to give you money and I didn't try to give it to you," she pointed out reasonably, even knowing that explanation wasn't going to work.

"Semantics." Trace came up behind her to pat her bottom. "Upstairs. Clothes off. Sit and wait for us on the bed."

With a low groan, Lila slowly moved upstairs and did as they'd ordered. After what seemed like hours, they entered the bedroom.

As one, they all dropped down to one knee before her. She stood there buck-naked, her mouth open as she gaped at them.

"Lila Richards," Gavin began. "I love you with all my heart. Each night when I come home, sometimes so tired I can hardly keep my eyes open, all I have to do is hear your laugh or see your smile or catch your scent and suddenly I'm filled with energy. You've brought laughter and fun back into my life. I love you, baby, will you marry me?"

Tears dripped down her cheeks. "Yes," she cried. Standing,

Gavin drew her into his arms and kissed her. Then letting her go, he stepped back and sat on the bed.

Trace grabbed her hands, hold them tight. "Lila, letting you leave years ago was the hardest thing I ever had to do. I thought about you every day, about holding you, loving you and now that you're here I thank God every day. I love you. Marry me?"

"Yes, oh yes." She leaped at him, knowing he'd catch her. He fell back on the bed with a laugh as she kissed his cheeks, his lips and the tip of his nose.

"Hey now, save some of that sugar for me, Lila," Colin teased.

Trace helped her stand and it was Colin's turn to take her hands. "Lila, you've shown me that I can have it all. No matter what was thrown your way, you've remained strong and sweet and you've kept us all sane. You've made my dreams come true and I love you. Will you do me the honor of being my wife?"

"Hmm, let me think," she teased, squealing as he grabbed her, tickling her.

"I give in, I give in, I'll marry you," she gasped, laughing as he laid her on the bed beneath him, resting his weight on his arms and kissing her passionately.

"You guys are more than I ever thought I deserved," Lila told them. "Some days I pinch myself just to make sure I'm not dreaming. I would love nothing more than to marry all of you." She pursed her lips. "How exactly does that work?"

"Technically, you'd marry Gavin since he's the oldest," Colin explained. "But we'd all be included in the ceremony and you'd be married to all of us in our hearts."

"Oh, that's nice."

"I'm glad you approve," Gavin rumbled in his deep voice. "How long do you think you'll need to plan this? One month?"

She punched his arm. "A year."

"Three months," he countered.

"Six months," she told him with a glare.

"Deal." He held out his hand and she giggled as she shook it.

"I can't believe we just negotiated when we were getting married. You're so romantic."

"We're not risking you ever getting away from us, baby. You're ours."

"Forever," Colin added.

"And even after that," Trace said.

"Yours. All yours."

Thanks for reading Lila's Loves! I hope you enjoyed it.
Read on for excerpts from the other books in the Haven, Texas series.

LAKEN'S SURRENDER

Haven, Texas, Book Two

"Morning, sugar."

Laken ground her teeth, telling herself it was annoyance and not pleasure she felt bubbling through her stomach.

Without looking up, she snapped back. "Don't call me that."

"Now, is that any way to greet a man bearing gifts?" he chided softly.

The old Duncan would have pulled her up for her tone of voice. The old Duncan would have bent her over the counter, scolding her as he smacked her butt. Or he would have ordered her to her knees and given her mouth something to occupy itself with.

That was something she did not miss.

So why do I keep goading him on? Why do I keep pushing, hoping for a reaction? Is there a part of me that wants him to take back control?

She squashed that voice as she glanced up. He was holding a brown paper bag and a large coffee. Her stomach growled. She knew what was in that bag. An apple turnover.

Her favorite.

"I'm not hungry."

His dark gaze narrowed as he looked her over.

"You've had breakfast?" he asked.

It entered her head that she could lie, but she'd never managed to successfully pull that off with him. He'd always known when she was lying.

"I'm not hungry," she repeated. "You know, you might want to get your ears cleaned out. I've heard wax build-up can make you really deaf."

Duncan placed the bag on the counter and leaned closer. Laken forced herself to stand her ground even as his scent surrounded her. Hot, molten male. Her insides quivered.

"You're losing weight you didn't have to lose, Laken. You need to take better care of yourself." He ran his thumb under her eye. For a brief moment she leaned into him before pulling back. "You have bags under your eyes. Your light was on late last night, can't you sleep?"

Her gaze shot up to meet his concerned one. She blushed, remembering how she hadn't bothered to pull down her drapes last night. Most evenings she was so worn out by the time she got to bed that she barely managed to find the energy to brush her teeth. She worked all day in her store, then spent hours at night working on new designs. Some days she didn't even leave the building.

"Spying on me, deputy?" She winced at the breathy tone of her voice as she glared at him.

He winked, giving her a quick grin. Her breath caught. He didn't smile often, but when he did... well it would take a stronger woman than her to resist the appeal of that smile.

"I was on duty last night. I just happened to be driving past."

That was not disappointment she felt. It was *not.*

"Well, go stalk someone else," she sniped, inwardly wincing at the acid in her tone. "I don't need or want you looking out for me."

"You're wrong, Laken," he said in a deep voice. "You need me more than you realize. Something's wrong and I want to know what it is. You're not eating or sleeping. You're snapping at everyone, even those just trying to help you. Keep up this heavy workload you're subjecting yourself to and you're going to end up in the hospital."

She snorted. "Don't you think you're being a bit overdramatic? Plenty of people work long hours, Duncan. Do you go around lecturing all of them?"

Duncan sighed. "Why are you so angry at me, Laken? I know I made mistakes years ago. I was too caught up in my career to give you the attention you deserved. Don't you think I deeply regret that? But I wasn't the only one who made mistakes. You never even gave me a proper explanation for why you broke things off. I think you owe me that much, don't you?"

"I told you why. Things weren't working out." She couldn't meet his eyes. "Do we have to rehash this over and over? You're like a bad batch of chili; you just keep repeating yourself. We're over, Duncan, we have been for years, and it's time you moved on with your life. I have."

Pain tore through her, but she forced herself to keep calm. She couldn't handle Duncan right now. He had always been a force to reckon with and if he set his sights on something then he would let nothing get in his way. It was that determination and drive that had made him a hugely successful linebacker.

She couldn't afford to have him focus all his attention on her. Because she had secrets that she was determined no one would ever uncover.

"You never could lie very well," he told her. "I'm not sure what is going on with you, but I do know that I missed you. A lot." He took hold of her hand. "I want us to try again. Go out on a date with me, Laken."

This was the third time he'd asked her on a date. Each time was harder than the last to say no.

She pulled her hand free, clenching her teeth against the initial surge of pleasure. A "yes" hovered on her lips. God, how easy it would be to fall back into Duncan's arms. But she couldn't get involved with him. Duncan would never let her secrets lie.

"I'm not doing this again. I'm not going to be your doormat."

His eyes grew cold. "You were never my doormat and you know it. What we did was always consensual and you loved being my submissive. You can spit and snarl at me all you like, but I am not giving up on you. Not this time. I learn from my mistakes, Laken. I would cherish you."

"Would you give up BDSM for me?" Christ, how had that slipped out? She wasn't even sure that was what she wanted. The thought of playing with Duncan again filled her with fear and longing. It was a sickening mix that made her head ache and her whole body throb.

He gazed at her thoughtfully. "Now why would you want me to do that? You loved being my submissive. Does this have something to do with why you broke things off? Did something happen to make you afraid of submitting to me, Laken?"

Christ, this is what she got for letting down her guard. She couldn't let Duncan close and keep her secrets.

Printed in Great Britain
by Amazon

25252005R00118